DEATH IN THE ENGLISH COUNTRYSIDE

DEATH IN THE ENGLISH COUNTRYSIDE

COUNTRYSIDE

BOOK ONE IN THE MURDER ON LOCATION SERIES

SARA ROSETT

DEATH IN THE ENGLISH COUNTRYSIDE
Book One in the *Murder on Location* series
Published by McGuffin Ink

Copyright © 2014 by Sara Rosett
Second Paperback Edition: October 2016
First Paperback Edition: September 2014
ISBN: 978-0998253503
Cover Design: Alchemy Book Covers

 Created with Vellum

"Angry people are not always wise."
-Pride and Prejudice

CHAPTER 1

LOS ANGELES

*E*VERYONE KNOWS MR. Darcy doesn't exist—he's a fictional character, after all—but that doesn't stop women from dreaming of their own personal wet shirt and/or "dearest Elizabeth" moment, something I'd forgotten as I pushed in through the door to Premier Locations. I was focused on the screen of my camera, flicking through the photos I'd taken that morning, gorgeous shots of hot air balloons suspended over the rolling hills of Temecula's wine country, and didn't look up as I navigated the three steps forward and one to the right, which brought me to my desk.

At Premier Locations our website motto was "Hollywood's leading location company," which was more wishful thinking than reality. We didn't have a lobby with plush chairs and a starlet-in-waiting functioning as a receptionist. No, we were as stripped down as an office could be. Three desks without cubicles were wedged into the "outer office" area. Two walled offices at the back of the space, one for our office manager Marci and the other for the owner Kevin, boasted actual doors that closed, but still lacked privacy due to the flimsy pressboard construction. The lights were on in Marci's office, but her desk was empty. Next door, Kevin's office was dark. He was currently scouting locations in England with the director of our newest project, a feature film adaptation of *Pride and Prejudice*.

"Finally, you're in." Lori, our intern, spun her office chair toward me, which sent her auburn hair spinning out like she was in a shampoo commercial. "So was he your Mr. Darcy?"

I transferred the straps of my tote bag from my shoulder to the back of my chair. "What?"

Lori popped the rings closed on a production notebook and rolled her eyes. "Jake, your date last night. Do you think he's your Mr. Darcy?"

Since Premier Locations had landed a project to find locations for a new *P & P* movie, Elizabeth Bennet, Jane Austen, and Mr. Darcy had become frequent topics at the office.

I snorted. "Definitely not Darcy."

My mother had asked me to meet her for dinner last night after work. I thought it was a spur-of-the-minute meeting.

I shouldn't have been so naïve. It's never just dinner with my mother.

I continued to skip through the photos, already mentally sorting them into categories for the website catalogue of potential locations.

She always has an agenda, which usually involves me in white tulle and the *Wedding March*. I suppose I should be glad she'd regained her equilibrium after my father announced he wanted a divorce because he was quitting his management job at the bank and moving to Kansas City to buy out an independent bookstore owner.

My father's departure had forced my mom to join the workforce, albeit reluctantly. She worked part-time at my uncle's event planning company, mostly coordinating weddings, which left plenty of time for her favorite hobby, ambush matchmaking—with me as the sole focus of her sideline interest.

Thus, the dinner invitation last night, in which she'd given me an air kiss, introduced the young man she'd somehow manipulated into being there, and fled. Lori had accompanied me to the Thai restaurant to pick up her to-go dinner order and had witnessed the whole awkward event.

I removed the memory card from my Canon and uploaded the images.

"Are you sure?" Lori asked. "He looked dreamy enough to be Mr. Darcy."

"Only if Mr. Darcy is twenty-eight, lives in an apartment above his mother's garage, and plays video games all day."

"Oh."

"Yeah. Oh."

"Well, I'm sure he's out there for you. Your Darcy, I mean."

"I hope so, but I'm seriously beginning to wonder." A few years ago, I would have agreed without a second thought. An Austen aficionado from the moment I cracked open *Pride and Prejudice* at fourteen years old, I was enthralled with her world and the characters she'd created, especially witty Elizabeth and prickly Mr. Darcy. When I first read Darcy's line stating how much he ardently admired and loved Elizabeth, I was sunk, pulled into the idea of a man who loves so completely that he goes against all barriers to be with her.

But now...well, I was beginning to wonder if that kind of love existed in the twenty-first century. "I've discovered that candidates with even a smidgeon of Mr. Darcy-like potential are extremely thin on the ground in modern Los Angeles."

"But there really is someone for everyone—my trig teacher who had halitosis and hardly ever wore matching socks was married. If that doesn't prove that there's someone for everyone, I don't know what does. You just haven't found your true love yet. You know, you're always dating those corporate types with their briefcases and smartphones, who barely have time for you. Maybe you should mix it up—go for someone a little less buttoned-down, more scruffy."

I thought of last week, sitting at the linen-covered table in La Pomodoro, waiting for Terrance and the text he'd finally sent: *Can't get away. Reschedule?*

"I don't always date corporate guys. I went out with Jeff for a while, remember? The medical intern."

"Wasn't he the one who fell asleep while you were in Starbucks?"

"Yes." I sighed. I'd been in the middle of recounting a story about how I got lost in a scary part of downtown L.A. when I looked up and saw his chin was propped on his hand, and he was asleep—eyelid-fluttering REM sleep.

"And then there was that real estate guy, what was his name?" Lori tilted her head to the side. "Why can't I remember it? His face is on billboards all over Santa Barbara."

"Tommy." I made a vow to never talk about my dating life again at the office. "*He* never fell asleep on me." But we were never actually able to complete a conversation because he was constantly on the phone. Open houses, escrow accounts, inspection dates—it was always an important call that he had to answer.

"See what I mean," Lori said, "They're all," she shifted her shoulders as she searched for the word she wanted, "so white collar-ish. You know, the first A.D. on that shoot a few weeks ago, Finn, he was interested in you, I could tell. I think you should reconsider that rule you have about never dating someone in the industry. Especially in Finn's case."

"You know how crazy our kind of work is. Can you imagine trying to fit in a date with someone else whose work is just as insane as ours?" Eighteen-hour days were the rule, not the exception for us, and the only fixed thing about our work schedules were that they were constantly changing. "No, it's better to keep things on a purely professional level with colleagues. And I'm not going to apologize for having standards. I mean, is it too much to ask that the guy I date have a job—a good job?"

"Finn has a good job."

"But he works in the industry, too. It would be better if I found someone who worked somewhere else. And before you say anything, it's not just about where he works. I want a guy who is smart and funny and responsible and—"

"You're too picky," Lori said. "Love is messy and complicated. You can't shove it in a spreadsheet."

"Says the woman without a boyfriend." I smiled to take any sting out of my words, and Lori laughed.

"Okay. That's true. But only temporarily. There's this hot guy at the gym. He's always on the treadmill at six-thirty." Lori grabbed another production notebook and flipped through the pages. "All I'm saying is that you should never rule out love."

The door opened, and Marci whipped into the office, her delicate filigreed chandelier earrings contrasting sharply with her tight T-shirt, low-cut jeans, and combat boots. "Oh good. You're back, Kate," she said as she passed my desk. "We need to talk in my office." Marci was a whirlwind, a four-foot-eleven tornado of energy. I grabbed my Moleskine notebook and jumped up to follow her. Marci had never been anything but nice to me, but I'd never given her any reason not to be.

The first week I went to work for Kevin as his assistant, I'd heard Marci on the phone chewing out a vendor who bailed on a shoot, and I'd decided I didn't want to ever be in her black books. Rumor around the office was that she had three tattoos, but no one had been brave enough to ask her about them; even normally fearless Zara, the other location scout in our office, had passed on that one. We did know Marci was divorced because she mentioned her ex once, saying that the world was better off without him, which Lori took to mean that Marci killed him. I thought that was ridiculous—well, most of the time I thought it was ridiculous.

Marci dropped a pile of three-ring binders on her desk, straightened her neon green, rectangular glasses, and closed the door behind me.

I raised my eyebrows. In the whole three years I'd worked for Premier Locations I'd never seen either her or Kevin's office door closed.

"Yes, it's bad." She sank into her chair and ran her fingers through her spiky brown hair that was sprinkled with white. Her hair needed a trim and she looked rather like an aging porcupine. "I haven't heard from Kevin in three days."

She'd kept her voice low, to compensate for the flimsy walls and lack of soundproof doors, so I scooted forward on the chair, inching nearer the desk.

I wasn't sure how to respond. "Is that...unusual?"

Kevin, Zara, and I worked independently. We were in and out of the office all the time and didn't keep tabs on each other.

"He finished with Mr. O'Leary and the rest of the group on Friday. Mr. O'Leary's return flight was earlier than Kevin's so he had a car pick him up and take him to the airport. Kevin was supposed to check out of the hotel Friday morning, drive the rental car back to London, and catch a late afternoon flight that would arrive here Friday night. After a trip, if he's not going to be in the office he checks in with me and sends me any files we need to upload to the server."

I nodded. We were an all-digital office. Clients accessed files through our secure server. Marci handled Kevin's uploads. The rest of us did our own for each project.

"When he didn't call this morning, I figured he was busy. Typical Monday, you know." She glanced at the clock. It was two in the afternoon. "But then I got a call from Mr. O'Leary's office. His assistant says he's anxious to see the new stuff that

Kevin promised him and that Mr. O'Leery is ready to be impressed." Marci shrugged. "I don't know what he's talking about. I don't have anything. Apparently, Kevin promised him something amazing, but hasn't uploaded it to the server or sent it to me. At lunch, I ran by his condo. I have a key so I can pick up his mail." She waved her hand at her key ring. "He's not back. His Saab isn't in his parking space. The blinds were closed, his mail was stacked up in his box, and his suitcase and the go-bag were gone."

"Oh." I sat back. The go-bag contained everything we needed to shoot while we were traveling. If the go-bag was gone, then Kevin was still gone. "And he's not one to be very neat. If he'd been back, you'd know it."

"He's not answering his cell." She took off her glasses and massaged the bridge of her nose. "I called the airline and checked his confirmation number. His return ticket wasn't used, and he's not at the hotel. The desk clerk said he checked out on Friday morning, but left his bags in storage with them, saying he would be back. They're still holding his things in their luggage storage room." She raised one hand, palm up, as she shrugged a shoulder. "He's disappeared."

"That's crazy. Why would he drop out of sight? Especially with Mr. O'Leery waiting for files?" I didn't know the details of the finances at Premier Locations, but you didn't have to be a genius to realize that the active project list was a lot shorter now than a few months ago. Kevin, not someone who usually showed excessive emotion, had been ecstatic when he landed the *P & P* project, reminding me of George Bailey at the end of *It's a Wonderful Life*, which I took to mean that things were even more precarious for our little company than I'd realized. The *P & P* job was huge—preliminary scouting, like the trip he was on, as well as doing the location management. It would certainly replenish the coffers. Kevin wouldn't throw away such a big project. "He wouldn't just disappear."

Marci gave me a long, assessing look. In that instant I knew that she was aware of the secret Kevin tried so hard to keep quiet. I'd been aware of it, but I didn't think anyone else in the office knew about it.

An addiction is hard to hide from an assistant who is with you every minute of your workday.

I came to work for Kevin as his assistant, gradually learning the business before he promoted me to a location scout with my own clients. Most of the time I worked with him, he was a wonderful boss, focused and on-point, getting the shots we needed, cajoling people to open their homes to allow us on their property to film, sharing tips and tricks that he'd learned the hard way, or recounting stories of his ruckus-rousing, pre-digital, good old days when he worked on a weekly cop show and had to race to the 24-hour film development kiosk to get photos quickly.

But there had been one time when he'd slipped. One morning, he hadn't shown up for a meeting. I'd handled it, then gone to his condo, where I found him, limp and morose, staring at reruns, a gin bottle upended in the sink. The next day, he caught me in the parking lot to tell me thanks for checking on him. He said he was in touch with his sponsor and that I didn't have to worry—it wouldn't happen again. And then we were off, running through the schedule as if the previous day were as fake as some of the locations we helped create. I'd never been sure if Marci was aware of Kevin's issue, but there was no question about it now.

"You knew." I matched her quiet tone.

"Oh, yes. Even though he is good at controlling it, I figured it out." She glanced at the door. "Lori and Zara don't have any idea."

"You're sure Lori doesn't know?"

"She hasn't worked with him long enough."

"And Zara never worked with him one-on-one," I said. Zara had worked freelance before moving to our office last year.

Marci rolled her chair closer to the desk. "So you and I are the only people who know...the possibilities. We need to keep it that way."

"Okay. I've never breathed a word about it before. I'm not about to start now."

"I know. That's why you have to go find him."

"What? Me?"

"Yes, it has to be you. I need you to go to England. You're the only one I can trust. I can't go. I have to keep the lid on things here. I can run interference with Mr. O'Leery until you find out how bad it is. I told his assistant we're having computer issues, so that's bought us a little time. Once we know the situation, we'll do damage control."

I fell back in the chair. Marci was right. If she left and word got out about why...I glanced again at the closed door. Lori was on the phone, and the low murmur of her voice filled the silence in Marci's office. If it became known that Kevin had gone on a bender—while working with a client, no less—business for Premier Locations would dry up. Hollywood reveled in stories of celebrities brought low by their own bad behavior, which generated buzz and raised movie stars' profiles, but movie- and television-making was a business. If Kevin Dunn was regarded as unreliable, Premier Locations was done.

"You don't think we should call the police?" I asked.

"I considered it, but what would we tell them? That he's not answering his phone and missed his flight? You know one of the first questions they'll ask is if it has happened before. What would I say? That he has a history of...erratic behavior, to put it nicely?" Marci shook her head. "If we go that way, then it's official with reports and questions and interviews."

"And records of inquiries and possible publicity."

"And you know how Mr. O'Leery feels about publicity, especially at the beginning of a film."

I blew out a breath. "He detests it."

"I can't jeopardize this project. If you go over there and can't...find him, if he's truly missing, we'll contact the police."

"Right. Yes, of course you're right." I sat up straight in the chair, running through my mental schedule. "But I've got a meeting in Palm Springs tomorrow. I finally got in touch with the owners of that ranch house that we're hoping to use for the sports drink ad."

"I'll take care of everything here." Marci swiveled her computer monitor toward me. "There's a flight out tonight. I think you should be on it."

A burst of laughter from Lori sounded from the other side of the door. I chewed the inside of my lip, running through mental arguments and discarding them as quickly as they came up. The sports drink company was my baby. I'd worked with them since their first tiny print ad. Now they were doing a full-scale marketing push—print, television, and Internet. They'd never worked with anyone else at our firm, and Jo, their head marketing honcho, trusted me implicitly.

I wanted to suggest that Zara or Lori go, but Zara had eight-year-old Darwin to take care of. She couldn't leave town on the spur of the moment, and as much as I loved Lori, she'd never traveled farther than San Diego. Did she even have a passport? And, discretion wasn't exactly a watchword with her. She tweeted, texted, and Instagrammed her breakfast choices. Entrusting her with the secret would be the equivalent of sending a press release to *E! News*.

"You're right. It has to be me." I took my phone out of my pocket, already mentally sorting through the people I needed to contact about my unexpected travel plans. My fingers flew over the keypad, tapping out messages. Then I made a to-do list in my Moleskine notebook topped with "pack umbrella."

Scouting and managing locations was all about the details. Almost everyone I knew relied on their phone to keep track of everything, but I was more old school. I kept the minutiae of my life in my Moleskine. Its battery never died, and I didn't have to worry about it being stolen or accidentally locking myself out by messing up my passcode.

"Thank you, Kate. I owe you big-time," Marci said. "I'll take care of everything in Palm Springs; just send me the details." Marci turned her monitor back so that it was facing her and began typing. "Manchester is closer to the little village where Kevin went, but London is the easier connection—there's more flights. You'll have to rent a car and drive, like Kevin did."

"Just remember this when you write the bonus checks at Christmas," I said as the printer hummed.

Marci shot me a smile as she handed me the still-warm pages. "Let's not go overboard. That is Kevin's itinerary, contact details for the local scout he worked with over there, and Kevin's hotel details. Now, what time do you want your flight? Is eight too early?"

She made the reservations, printed my boarding pass, and I returned to my desk to send her the wine country photos. The door banged open again, and Zara, entered. "Mail call," she announced. I grabbed a padded envelope that came flying through the air toward me.

Lori snagged a small cardboard box that went wide of her. "If this is Kevin's new lens, you'd better be glad I was the best shortstop on my softball league." She carefully put down the box and asked, "how was your trip? I forgot to ask this morning."

Zara was marching to her desk, her thick clogs thudding along the floor, but for an instant she checked her stride and gave Lori a sharp look. "What? I didn't go on a trip."

"But I heard you on the phone last week with your friend,

asking if she could drop you at the airport and keep Darwin for you. Where'd you go?"

There was a second's pause. I looked up from my computer screen. Zara never thought before she spoke. She had no filter, but if I didn't know her as well as I did I would have thought she looked worried. But Zara didn't worry—about anything. She raced through life, never fretting over anything or second-guessing herself. "Oh, that," she said breezily. "My ex. Causing legal trouble, yet again. I had to take a couple of personal days and fly to Chicago to get it straightened out." Her desk chair squeaked as she dropped into it. "Never get married, Lori. That's my advice. That way, you never have to get divorced." She glanced above Lori's head to the three movie posters from the recent film and mini-series versions of *Pride and Prejudice* that Lori had pinned on the wall. "Not what dear Jane would advise, I know, but that's the way I see it. So, what's going on this afternoon? We're not talking true love again, are we?"

The news about Kevin was all I could think of at the moment. I mentally groped about for some innocuous topic, but I should have known Lori would fill the conversational gap. "Why shouldn't we talk about love?" She raised her chin. "It's what *P & P* is about."

Zara opened a file on her computer. "It's about money."

"You said you'd never watched it." Lori sounded like a lawyer during cross-examination.

"I said I didn't *like* it, not that I'd never watched it." Keeping her eyes on the screen, Zara clicked away as she talked. "If we're keeping score, or something, I've also read the book. Not the manga version, either."

"There's a manga version? Cool," Lori said with respect. "But that's not what we're talking about. The point is, Elizabeth doesn't marry Darcy for his money. She loves him."

Zara looked at me and sighed. "I try and tell her that life isn't all long stemmed roses and happily ever after, but does she listen to me? Cold hard cash makes the world go round. That's how it is now, and that's how it was in Austen's day."

Before I could reply, Lori said, "You can't tell me you didn't fall for Darcy...just a little bit, if not in the books, then in the wet shirt scene?"

"Oh, forget Mr. Darcy." Zara ducked her cropped head of dark hair as she shifted through the stacks of paper on her desk. "I'm sick of Mr. Darcy. Give me Wickham any day."

Lori sucked in her breath. "Zara! He's a cad."

"Well, he'd certainly be more fun than stuffy, repressed Darcy." Zara pulled out one of the pages from the bottom of a stack and shook it at Lori. "Rakes are always more fun."

Lori narrowed her eyes. "You only want to get a rise out of me. Come on, Kate, back me up. You studied all this stuff for your doctorate. Mr. Darcy is the one you want to end up with forever, right? Not some deceptive liar."

"I don't have a doctorate. Far from it, actually."

Lori swished her hand through the air as if several classes and an unfinished dissertation were minor details. "Kevin says you're our English Lit expert. He's adamant that you'll be on the *P & P* team when he gets back. Because of your background knowledge, he said."

"He will need an assistant," I agreed, trying to keep my tone normal and not act as if I knew that our boss had seemingly disappeared into a black hole. "I can't deny that I'm looking forward to wallowing in Jane Austen and the Regency and getting paid for it."

"It's those breeches, isn't it?" Zara said with a lift of an eyebrow. "You know you could still go back and finish your degree. Your dissertation could be called the Power of Pants. I swear that's why all those movies are so popular. It's because of those form-fitting breeches."

"We're not talking about pants," Lori said. "We're talking

about love. I can't believe you'd even think of picking Wickham over Darcy. She's crazy, isn't she, Kate?"

"Mr. Darcy is better husband material than Wickham, I'll give you that." I clicked my mouse, sending the details for the sports drink ad to Marci. "Although, I've always thought the fencing scene was much sexier than the wet shirt scene. And you know there are other Austen heroes like Mr. Tilney, Mr. Knightley, and Colonel Brandon. Not everyone finds brooding attractive. Why haven't any of her other heroes taken off in popular culture?"

"Because they didn't have a wet shirt scene," Zara said.

I shut down my computer, shouldered my tote bag, and headed for the door. "There's a lot more to Austen than wet shirt scenes."

A call came in from my mother as I walked through the parking garage to my car. She'd obviously gotten my text.

"You can't go out of town," she said. "You have to come to dinner on Tuesday. I've already invited my new neighbor. Twenty-four B—a corner condo on the top floor, one of the most expensive condos in the building. You know he's well-off."

"Mom. I'm dating Terrance."

"It never hurts for a man to have a little competition. Besides, you're not dating him. You two simply text back and forth. That's not a relationship. All you do is plan to meet, then reschedule."

I blew out a calming breath. "You've been in my phone again."

"I had to make a call the other day at lunch when you were in the restroom. My battery was low. I can't help it if a text came in while I was on the phone. Of course, I looked at it."

"And through all my old messages, too." I reached my car and tossed my tote bag in the passenger side of my ten-year-old black Accord then slammed the door harder than necessary. The noise reverberated off the concrete, drowning out my mother's voice for a few seconds.

"...thirty-six, single, and a veterinarian. Just broke up with his girlfriend, and has a nice head of hair—thick, not thinning like so many men in their thirties."

"Does he have all his own teeth, too?"

"I don't know." She'd completely missed my sarcasm. "I'm sure I can find out," she said, her tone serious.

The absurdity of our conversation hit me, and I shook my head, a little laugh escaping.

"Are you laughing? I don't know why. These things are important."

My relationship with my mom was one of those situations where I had to find the humor in it—or it would drive me crazy. "Mother, your skills are wasted in wedding planning. You know that, don't you?"

"I'm sure I don't know what you're talking about."

"You should be a matchmaker." I walked around to the driver's side. "You'd probably make a fortune. Or you should go to work for the NSA. No one can ferret out information like you." I held open the door, letting the heat escape.

"I know what you're trying to do, change the subject, but I'll not rise to the bait. Dinner, Tuesday. Let's say seven."

"No, Mother. I can't. I'll be out of the country." That excuse stunned her into silence for a moment. "You have dinner with your vet," I said. "He sounds wonderful. Maybe you should date him."

"Katherine! That's—I could never. I mean—I'm sure I don't know what to say."

"He's not that much younger than you. I have to pack. Love you. I'll text you."

My name echoed through the parking garage and turned to see Marci trudging my way, waving a cell phone. "Take this. It's got a SIM card that will work over there."

Kevin had a drawer full of burner phones and country-specific SIM cards.

Marci continued, "I sent an email to the local guy Kevin used over there, Alex Norcutt. Told him you were arriving."

"Good idea. I'll contact him when I get there." We often used someone local to help us when we worked out of town. He could tell me exactly where he took Kevin.

"I'll contact the hotel, tell them we're sending someone to pick up Kevin's stuff. Keep me updated," Marci said.

"Of course." I leaned into the car and tossed the phone into my tote bag.

Instead of walking quickly away, Marci lingered then surprised me by catching me up into a tight hug. "You be careful, kid."

I come from a long-line of personal-space-respecting, non-hugging people, so I froze for a second, but her unexpected concern took away my reserve. I patted her shoulder tentatively and stepped back. "I will."

I moved to the car, then paused, my hand on the hot metal. "You know, he'll probably turn up tomorrow, and you'll have paid for a ticket to England for no reason."

"Yeah, I know," Marci said, but her tone contradicted her words.

CHAPTER 2

THE PLANE LANDED AT THREE in the afternoon, London time. After ten hours in the air, I wanted a shower and a change of clothes, but I made my way to the rental car counter instead. When I wasn't napping during the flight or reading the Agatha Christie book I'd brought, I'd read the paperwork that Marci had given me, which included Kevin's travel plans. He'd rented a car at the airport, picked up Mr. O'Leery, who flew in the same day as Kevin, and then had driven to the village they were using as their base. According to Marci's notes, the director of photography and the production manager were both based in England and planned to meet Kevin and Mr. O'Leery in the village. The local scout had arranged for a van to shuttle all five of them around the countryside while looking at locations. Kevin planned to keep his rental car during the duration of his stay, then return it to the airport before his return flight.

I figured I'd retrace Kevin's steps. A best-case scenario would be that I would run across him as he made a delayed return route to the office. Or, even better, I'd discover he was already on his way home, and our paths had crossed in the air over the Atlantic.

Marci had booked him a mid-size four-door sedan to be picked up at the airport last Tuesday, the day of his arrival. Normally, a scouting trip for a feature film, even a preliminary scouting trip, would involve quite a few people, and we often booked vans to accommodate our luggage and gear. We could get a lot done on the road and used the hours in the car as work time, but Mr. O'Leery was eccentric. Famous for being extremely guarded and secretive, he insisted on complete security at the beginning of his projects. Rumors even hinted there was a slight touch of paranoia about him. He had required that the first scouting trip consist of only himself, Kevin, the director of photography, and the production manager.

A woman wearing an ascot and a perfunctory smile greeted me at the rental car counter. I squared my shoulders and put on my brightest smile.

"I need to check on this rental from last week." I consulted the papers and read off the reservation number. "Has it been returned?"

As the woman with the ascot clacked away on the keyboard, another woman, this one younger, entered the area behind the counter, knotting her scarf and tucking it into her neckline as she moved.

The woman helping me glanced behind her. "You're late," she said, then turned back to me, and switched on a quick, apologetic smile. "And your name?"

"Kate Sharp." The new woman, her ascot now crooked, but in place, squinted her eyes at the other woman's back. While the woman helping me studied the computer screen, I exchanged a sympathetic look with the new arrival. I knew what it was like to work with self-important morons who made everyone else's life miserable. Months working as a temp had left an indelible impression on me.

Miss Perfect Ascot's smile disappeared. "I'm sorry, but you're not on this reservation. Do you have another confirmation number?"

"I know I'm not on that reservation. It was for my boss, Kevin Dunn. I work for Premier Locations." I put a business card on the counter. "I need to know if his car was returned." I figured Kevin's name wasn't well known—not like Mr. O'Leery's. It couldn't hurt to ask out-right about the status of the car.

She looked at the card, blinked a few times, her smile now fixed. "We have a corporate privacy policy. I'm sure you understand."

I checked my watch and did some quick mental math. In L.A. it was seven in the morning. Marci wouldn't be in the office yet, and I didn't have her cell phone number.

I could hear Kevin's voice in my head. "Going in straight isn't working for you, is it?"

Kevin was a genius when it came to convincing people to do what he wanted. I had been terrible at it when I first went to work for him. I didn't like asking people for things like permission to look at their house or shoot on their property, but I disliked working as a temp even more. So to keep my job as Kevin's assistant, I'd learned to ask, to push just a little, but more than that—I'd also learned that it was important to figure out what a person wanted.

I'd forgotten one of Kevin's first lessons—assess the person and develop a strategy. Kevin was the master of visual assessments. Where Kevin had a Sherlockian ability to give someone a once-over and come up with a weak point, I had been clueless—at least when I first went to work for him. I'd learned a lot about reading people from Kevin. Sometimes a couple of folded bills handed over discreetly did the trick, but other times fawning or flirting were required. To hone my skills in the assessment department, as he called it, we used to bet on the weak point. The first time it happened, we'd found a perfect location for a sports gear ad, a stretch of rural land with rolling hills off a California highway that had a thoroughbred, back East feel to it, the look the director wanted.

The owner, a woman in her early seventies, had refused point-blank to even talk to Kevin. He'd had a ten-second glimpse of her before she shut her front door in his face. He'd turned to me and asked what I thought would get her to come around.

"Nothing?"

"Oh ye of little faith. No, she has something she wants. Everyone wants something. Sometimes it's money, but not always. Recognition, approval, consideration, even flirting, those are all things people want as well. What do you think she wants?"

"To be left alone."

"Well, sure, she does right now, but go beyond this moment."

"Umm, money?"

Kevin laughed. "Did you see those clothes? Cotton T-shirt and worn jeans, both designer brands? Money is the last thing she wants. Last thing she needs, actually. She's got plenty of it already."

"How do you know that?"

"She's got enough money that she doesn't care how she looks—a look that only old-money people have. Usually it's the *nouveau riche* who want to flaunt their wealth. Don't make the mistake of offering money the moment someone blocks you." Kevin waved a hand. "Look around. What do you see?"

"A ranch-style house, probably sixty years old, a barn, a paddock, and miles of split-wood fence."

Kevin waited expectantly. "Don't you see it?"

"What? She likes living in the country?"

"More than that. See how much nicer the barn is than the

house? She loves her horses. Did you notice the homemade water reclamation system on the side of the house? The hybrid car with the canvas bags in the back seat?"

I scanned the property. "And she has oversized recycling bins along the driveway. She's into the green movement."

Kevin nodded. "A real back-to-nature person who would probably be thrilled to help out a company..." Kevin said in a leading tone of voice.

"Dedicated to those same principles," I finished, excitedly.

"Exactly."

We'd returned a few days later with a canvas shopping bag with the company's logo on it and a report detailing how the company adhered to green ideals. I could tell Kevin had her interest before he got through his first few sentences.

I'd gone in cold at the rental car counter. My mistake. I ran a critical eye over the woman and decided money wasn't her kryptonite. A canvas shopping bag wouldn't sway her either. My professional assessment was that a designer leather handbag would unlock the info on her computer screen, but that was out of the question with my bank account balance.

"I do have a reservation," I said while mentally casting around for ideas on how to make the situation work for both of us. I handed over the rental car reservation that Marci had booked for me when she purchased my airline ticket. While Miss Perfect Ascot banged away on the computer keyboard, I came up with a new strategy. I'd get my car then call the rental car company number. I bet they had an automated system, and I could punch in the confirmation code to get the basic details on the rental.

A buzzer sounded, and Miss Perfect Ascot let out a little huff of impatience when the other woman didn't immediately move to the back room. "Can you get that? I'm with a customer."

"You'd better go." The other woman twitched her scarf into

place and moved to the counter. "It's a delivery. I saw the bloke on my way in. You'll have to sign for it. You know, you being the manager, and all. I can't do that. Go ahead, I'll finish up here."

I signed in the appropriate places then followed the younger woman to the car, a red Golf hatchback. Marci certainly hadn't sprung for the luxury car, but then again, she'd just paid for a last-minute LAX to London airline ticket, which had to have cost an outrageous amount.

"I'd upgrade you," the woman said, "but I don't have anything else."

"Don't worry. This will be great." I looked doubtfully at the steering wheel positioned on the right. "That will take a bit of getting used to," I muttered to myself. On a lot of scouting trips, especially the early ones, I was the designated driver, which had nothing to do with alcohol. As the least senior person on the crew, it was my job to get us where we were going, which freed up Kevin and our clients to work during the drive. I'd done my share of driving in foreign countries, every-where from the barely-contained craziness of Mexico's roads to the super organized Autobahns of Germany, but I hadn't driven in England.

"Never driven on the left?" She opened the hatchback and handed me the keys.

"Nope. No time like the present."

"You'll do fine. It's an automatic."

"Thank goodness for that." I removed my GPS from my tote bag before I tossed it along with my tiny suitcase in the back and closed the hatch. I'd packed for this trip like any other scouting trip—light. Kevin was easy-going in most ways, but absolutely ferocious about luggage. Two bags—two *small* bags —were his limit. I'd looked at him doubtfully the first time I went out of town on a crew, but when I arrived at the airport and saw our luggage and gear arranged in a small foothill, I'd realized how smart he was.

As the woman handed me the paperwork for the car, she leaned a little closer. "That confirmation number you were curious about—still open. And being charged everyday it's not back."

"Thanks. I appreciate it." Sometimes all it took was a little sympathy to gain someone's cooperation.

She nodded and headed back to the counter. I started the car and adjusted the mirrors, then sat there for a moment, the kernel of worry growing as I thought about the bill adding up on the rental car. Kevin wasn't careless about the financial aspects of the business. He wasn't a tightwad—he'd spring for lunch for the office, and he always gave us Christmas bonuses —but he kept an eye on expenses. It was hard to imagine him letting the rental car charges continue to build.

I blew out a breath and decided I couldn't put it off any longer. I had to get on the road. I wanted to be in the village of Nether Woodsmoor before nightfall.

WITH THE HELP of the GPS and only three near heart attacks later, I had managed to stay on the correct side of the road and had negotiated away from the clogged roads of London to the clogged motorway that stretched north. Nether Woodsmoor was a small village located in the English countryside of Derbyshire and, according to our local location scout, ideally suited for a day's exploration of potential filming sites. Remembering the emails he and Kevin had exchanged, I had been careful to put the full name of the village into the GPS. Nether Woodsmoor was a completely different place than Woodsmoor, he'd cautioned.

The tall hedgerows sped by, and I caught a few glimpses of

thatched roofs, but my attention was more on the car and the road than the scenery until I drove over a wide, fast moving river into Nether Woodsmoor.

Cottages of honey-colored stone lined the narrow streets. The main road curved and brought me into the center of the village where I slowed to take in a tea shop with window boxes of flowers, stores with striped window awnings, and swinging signs poking out into the air advertising everything from pubs to a bike shop. A church in the same golden stone towered imposingly over a broad swath of green grass lined with flowerbeds. It was a perfect English village. I loved it from the moment I saw it and I bet Kevin did too.

I found the Old Woodsmoor Inn farther down the road beyond the church. A two-story white stucco and wood beamed building with leaded glass windows, the inn had been converted from a coaching inn to a boutique hotel.

Set back from the thoroughfare on a quiet stretch of the road, there were no other buildings around the inn, only rolling green fields stretching off into the distance and occasional bunches of trees. A series of low walls made of flat stones stacked on each other divided the fields into sections of varying shapes and shades of green.

I crossed the gravel parking area to a paved courtyard. Inside, wide plank boards creaked under my feet as I crossed to the reception desk under an exposed wood beam ceiling. Beyond the reception area, tables and bench seating ranged around the room. The inn was obviously a popular spot for dinner, and I quickly scanned the occupants of the tables for Kevin's oversized frame, but he wasn't at one of them, nor was he lounging in a chintz-covered armchair in front of a fireplace.

"May I help you?"

I turned my attention back to the desk where a guy of about

forty with thinning blond hair and a bulldog-like build, squat and sturdy, stood behind the counter.

I gave him my reservation details and added, "I'm with Premier Locations." I knew Kevin would have used the company's name, and he and Mr. O'Leery would have registered under their own names. There was no way you could keep a secret from the actual town where you were looking to film a movie. The best he and Mr. O'Leery could hope for was that the attention they drew remained local and didn't reach across the pond.

"Right. Right. The chap who got called away, unexpected like. Room Twelve."

I nodded a vague agreement. Marci had obviously spun a tale to cover for Kevin's no show.

He continued, "Got his stuff stashed away, all secure."

"Thanks, I appreciate it."

"I'll send it up to your room shortly. You're here for two nights?"

"Yes. Wrapping up a few things for Kevin." I pulled out my company credit card. "Did he leave anything open? Any incidentals that need to be paid? Bar tab, something like that?"

He checked the computer screen. "No. Didn't have time to run up any charges. Wasn't around here much."

"Really?"

"Yeah. He and his mates left early, stayed out all day."

"Did you happen to see him on Thursday or Friday?" I asked, striving for a casual tone.

"No, not him. One of his mates, the sickly-looking fellow, I saw him on Friday." I nodded, recognizing Mr. O'Leery from his description.

He continued, "I carried his bags out to his car. That was quite a sight for our little village—a fancy black limo picking up a bloke just to drive him to the airport. Posh."

He pushed a key across the counter to me. "You're in the next room along from where your colleague stayed, thirteen. I'm Doug. My wife Tara and I, we're the owners. Let us know if there's anything we can do for you." He tilted his head to the end of the L-shaped room. "Bar's around the corner and stays open until one. The restaurant opens for breakfast at seven-thirty." He came around the counter and picked up my small bag.

"So, Doug, what is there to do around here?"

"There're a couple of pubs down the road in the village proper. The White Duck is the closest. Food's good. Not as good as here." He smiled.

"Of course not."

"Got several grand houses close-by. Lots of nice trails for rambling. The closest is across the road. Bit of a climb up the hill, but a nice view at the top. If you like sport, we have a golf course over toward Brunner's Hill. And Roman ruins about twenty minutes up the road, too. After Easter, things pick up, but for now we're a quiet place."

"Sounds lovely." I followed him up a set of wooden stairs to a narrow hall decorated only with a carpeted runner. There wasn't room for anything else. The low ceiling and small doors reminded me how old the building was. Clearly, the whole place had been modernized and updated, but I felt the age of the building on the upper floor. I envisioned men in great coats and women in Regency bonnets, their skirts swishing along the floor, as they moved down this hallway.

"Here we are." Doug opened a door midway down the corridor. More chintz, this time an unusual pattern of flowers and parrots, provided bright accents in the room, which contained twin beds and a wardrobe in dark wood. He pushed open a door on the far side of the room. "En suite bath here."

"Looks wonderful. Thank you." I reached for my wallet for a tip, but he held up his hand.

"Not necessary. Just doing my job."

He was gone before I could insist. I sat down on the armchair positioned by the single window, which overlooked the front courtyard and gravel sweep, and consulted the paper with Kevin's rental car information. Marci hadn't gone cheap with him. She'd reserved him a car from the luxury tier, a sedan. He was traveling with Mr. O'Leery, so the nicer car was understandable.

I scanned the parking area. No luxury cars, but they might have given him a different car at the airport. I took out the temporary cell phone and sent a text to Marci, letting her know I'd arrived at the inn, and that there was no sign of Kevin. *Can you find out what kind of car he got at the airport? Color? Make? They didn't want to talk to me since my name wasn't on the reservation. Found out he hasn't returned the car yet, though.*

A tap on the door sounded. I opened it, and a teenage boy, who I assumed was Doug's son because of his shock of pale hair, brought a rolling suitcase and a large backpack into the room. I thanked him and closed the door, then stood there a moment, looking at the two bags. Of course, I'd expected Kevin's battered silver hard-sided case. It was the other bag that had thrown me. It was the go-bag. Where would Kevin go for days and *not* take the go-bag?

CHAPTER 3

ALWAYS TAKE THE GO-BAG. It was one of Kevin's golden rules. He didn't have tons of rules. He wasn't a nitpicky boss. The "no more than two bags when traveling" was one rule. Another was "always take the go-bag." His voice echoed in my head, "You never know when you'll need it. And I promise you, the time you don't take it—that's when you'll wish you had."

I crossed the room and slowly opened the backpack. It was filled with labeled zipper pouches containing our equipment. I ran my hands over the pouches, mentally checking them off. They were all there. The only thing missing was Kevin's trusty Canon.

I opened the suitcase next. His laptop sat atop a mess of haphazardly folded clothes. I set the laptop aside and shuffled through the clothes. It was the suitcase of a seasoned traveler—khaki and dark pants, an assortment of short- and long-sleeved shirts, all in fabrics that could be washed out in the sink and that would dry quickly, wrinkle free. A sport coat and a few ties were on the bottom of the suitcase. A mix of socks and underwear, a pair of sweats, and a shaving kit rounded out the items. Nothing earth shattering there. Except there was no jacket and no camera. I wasn't surprised about the camera. I was sure Kevin had it with him.

I went through the clothes again, then sat back on my heels, frowning. Knowing England's notoriously fickle weather, Kevin would not travel here without a waterproof jacket and an umbrella. I tried the laptop, but it was password protected, and my attempts to guess his password failed.

My cell phone buzzed with a text from Marci. *Glad you're there. No word here. K's rental was a black Mercedes. Keep me updated.*

I went to the window again. A few more cars had arrived, and one of them was a black Mercedes. I left the suitcase and backpack where they were and grabbed my black peacoat. Back in hot Southern California, I almost hadn't packed the wool coat, but I was glad I'd brought it. The breezy mid-sixty degree temperature felt down right cold. I shoved my wallet, room key, and temporary cell phone in my pocket. I was about to head downstairs, but I went back to my luggage and pulled out my personal cell phone, which I'd also brought with me. It was turned off to save on international roaming charges.

I turned it on and used the inn's Wi-Fi to check messages and texts. I deleted a long-winded voicemail from my mom reminding me about the dinner party. My mother tended to only hear what she wanted to and forgot everything else. I texted back. *Impossible. Out of the country.*

I also had several texts from Terrance. The first read, *R u here?* The next asked if he'd gotten the day or time wrong. I groaned and tapped out a quick reply. How had I forgotten to tell him that I was going out of town and couldn't make our rescheduled date for lunch at the sushi bar? I waited a few moments to see if he'd reply back, but he didn't, so I headed downstairs.

I passed through the reception area and took a quick look

around the restaurant and bar area, but didn't see Kevin. Maybe he'd just arrived.

I hurried across the courtyard to the gravel parking area. The black Mercedes sat at the far end of a row, angled into a spot on the grass that I bet wasn't meant to be a parking slot. As I got closer, I could see a sign posted on a tree directly in front of the Mercedes that read NO PARKING. *Typical Kevin*, I thought with a surge of relief. He did have an arrogant streak. He often double-parked or slipped into no parking zones.

I always protested when he did it, but he brushed me off saying, "That's not for us. That's no parking for *other people*."

As I neared the car, my steps slowed. Now that I was closer, I could see through the tinted windows to the backseat where I could make out the shape of a child's car seat and some toys.

It wasn't Kevin's car—it wasn't even a rental. I stood with my hands on my hips for a second, then blew out a breath and turned to the road. The inn was set a little distance beyond the main hub of activity in the village, but I could see the sign for the White Duck. It was twilight, but I could make the short walk into the village before the sun went down. I followed the well-worn path beside the road, passing the church and village green. The pub had heavy wooden beams on the ceiling and a stone fireplace that filled one wall. Copper pots decorated the walls along with chalkboards listing specials. A few people were scattered around the room, mostly near the fireplace.

No sign of Kevin, which was becoming a recurring theme. I studied the menu, ordered a shepherd's pie at the bar, paid with the pounds I'd exchanged at the airport, and found a quiet table near a window. When the waitress brought my food, I realized I hadn't eaten anything since the questionable pasta I'd had on the plane. My mouth watered at the sight of the toasted golden potatoes layered over meat and veggies. I dug in, consuming the whole thing in a truly unladylike fashion. The woman who'd taken my order at the bar circulated through the pub, wiping down tables. When she reached my table, she gestured to my plate, eyebrows raised. "Take that for you?"

"Yes. It was wonderful. Just flew in today, and I was starving after the airplane food."

She was a plump woman in her thirties. Her dark hair had a reddish tint to it, sort of a black cherry color. Long bangs dipped below her eyebrows while the rest of her hair was pulled back in a ponytail. She wore a green apron with the name LOUISE stitched on it. She grimaced. "That's not food."

"I couldn't agree more."

"You're American?"

"Just in from Los Angeles."

She paused, as I hoped she would, my empty plate in one hand, the bar towel in the other. I wasn't about to make the same mistake I'd made at the car rental counter and dive in asking questions. I hoped to pique her interest. Surely visitors from Los Angeles weren't all that frequent in Nether Woodsmoor?

"Are you with those other blokes? The movie people?"

Bingo. I tried to keep any eagerness out of my voice. It was no secret that Kevin and Mr. O'Leery were in England looking at locations, but I didn't want to get into why I was looking for Kevin. In this day of Internet communication, a single tweet could blow apart the careful fiction that Marci and I had constructed. Of course, Louise didn't look like the tweeting type, but you never knew. If there was one thing I'd learned being in and out of people's homes and lives was that people were endlessly surprising. For all I knew, Louise might run a popular blog and have tons of followers, so I only said, "Yeah, I know them through work." It was absolutely true. "One in particular. Tall, bulky guy with dark hair and a boisterous personality. Kevin. I heard he was here. Have you seen him?"

"Not lately." She looked out the window as she considered. "It's been several days since he came in. At least before the weekend." She pointed the towel at me. "It was Friday. Lunch crowd. Don't think he stayed long. You might ask Doug at the Inn. He'll know."

I said I'd do that and wondered how long it would take for the information to get back to her that I was a guest at that same inn. I hoped that news that I'd picked up Kevin's luggage wouldn't be included. It would look odd. I took a final sip of my water—I usually stuck to water after a long flight to rehydrate—and decided that I had to contact the local scout Kevin had worked with. I'd really thought I'd find Kevin snoring off an awful hangover in a dark corner of the pub. I'd started the trip feeling more exasperated with Kevin than worried about him, but now my level of worry was growing.

I pulled out my phone and realized I didn't have the local scout's phone number. It was back at the inn.

On my way out the door, I asked Louise if there were any more pubs in the area. "I want to visit as many as I can while I'm here."

She'd dropped off some pints at a table and wiped her hands on the bar towel as she answered. "The Peacock is around the corner. Then there's the King George. To get to it, go up the main road here to the river, then take a right on the street that runs alongside the river. That will take you to the King George." She pointed away from the river. "About five miles up the main road is the Coach and Horses. The Old Crown is beyond it."

I thanked her and left. It was fully dark when I emerged. The temperature had dropped with the sunset, and the cold air felt like a slap, but there were still a few people moving around the village on foot and in their cars.

I could feel the tiredness from the time change and the flight creeping up on me. My limbs felt heavy, but I had to check the other pubs. And I had to do it as soon as possible. The sooner I found Kevin, the sooner I could call Marci, and we could put an end to damage control. I walked up the street toward the river, passed closed shops and a few restaurants doing a desultory business. I bet that when summer came, there were café tables on the sidewalk filled with hikers and bikers.

I found The Peacock and took a quick peek inside. The low-ceiling room was crowded with tables, but there were only a few customers, none of whom were Kevin. I continued up the main street until I reached the river, then turned right and walked along the street that fronted the river. It was a pedestrian zone, a wide, paved area with benches spaced every few feet facing the water. Dark and opaque, the water swooshed by, creating a low, constant murmur in the night air.

I spotted the King George. Light from its windows fell across the benches by the water. I didn't even have to go inside the pub. I was able to look in the windows and see that Kevin wasn't there.

I dropped onto one of the benches to consider my options. I really didn't have any options. I had to check out the other pubs, but I wasn't eager to hit the road again. I delayed a few moments and watched the water as it swept by. I shivered. I bet the water was freezing, despite it being March. Even the Pacific wasn't actually warm this time of year, so a river in cool, rainy England was probably frigid.

A couple, cuddling and giggling, meandered by, then sharp and anxious words from another pair, this one mismatched in height, caught my attention. Light from the King George picked out the woman's grayish-brown hair and her busty figure, but didn't fall on the guy. He sounded young, and his nervous tone carried over the low murmur of the water. "...don't feel right about it now. Witnessing—"

The woman cut him off. "We've done nothing wrong. Remember that. Only signed a paper. No shame in that." She lowered her voice. "It will all work out, you'll see." Their words faded as they moved beyond me. The door of the pub opened and a group came out, debating the merits of driving to a restaurant in Upper Benning versus going to the inn where I was staying. The inn won out, and the group moved away.

I lugged myself up from the bench and followed the group back to the inn, but when they went inside for dinner, I got in the rental, steeled my nerves, and pulled out onto the road again, mentally chatting, *left, stay left*. I played follow the leader at the roundabouts, shadowing the cars in front of me as I fought my instincts to drive on the right.

I arrived at the Coach and Horses, sat at the bar, and ordered a basket of fries—chips in the local vernacular—and a Diet Coke, breaking my water-only rule, but I needed the caffeine. The place wasn't full, and it wasn't hard to work in a mention of Kevin into the conversation with the man behind the bar. He hadn't seen Kevin, but informed me that there was a new gastropub on the next street. I finished my chips, walked down the charming street of stone houses and shops, and had a look at the gastropub, which turned out to be the Old Crown that Louise had mentioned. I didn't even have to go in to know it wasn't the kind of place that appealed to Kevin. He didn't go in for fancy gourmet food. I made a quick trip in to ask about reservations. As I got my answers, I scanned the room. Kevin wasn't there, and the hostess-type kid didn't remember seeing him.

The caffeine from the soda helped me stay alert on the quiet drive back through the dark countryside. I put in plenty of long days, so I was used to pressing on through exhaustion, but I was glad when the car's headlights illuminated the sign for the inn. I checked the parking lot, but it was even emptier than it had been earlier. I could tell at a glance that there was no new black Mercedes.

I stifled a yawn as I waved a greeting to the blond-haired teen manning the reception desk and went up the narrow stairs, setting off a chorus of squeaks and groans as my feet hit the aged wood. I couldn't fight the jetlag anymore and felt as if I was moving in slow motion. I entered my cozy room and wanted to crawl into bed, but I needed to get in touch with the local scout...what was his name? I scrubbed my hand across my face and blinked hard to keep my eyes open as I searched the pile of papers Marci had given me. Alex. That was it. Alex Norcutt.

I didn't dare sit down on the bed before I contacted him, so I made myself stand while I tapped out a text, telling him I was in town and asking if he could meet with me in the morning. *I'll just curl up here for a little bit,* I decided, snuggling into the soft pillows on one of the twin beds. *See if he replies back.* I'd get up in a few minutes to unpack, change into my t-shirt and sleep pants, and take off my makeup.

I JERKED AWAKE, my heart thudding. Confused and disoriented, I looked around the strange room. A narrow column of sunlight streamed into the room through a gap in the heavy drapes. Parrot chintz.

Ah, yes. It all came back: England. Kevin missing. I looked at the clock. Hmm...my quick nap had turned into a twelve-hour marathon.

A knock sounded on the door, and I struggled into a sitting position. Had I ordered breakfast the night before? No, I was sure I hadn't. Sometime during the night I'd burrowed under the covers. I flung them back and swung my legs over the side of the bed. The knock sounded again, louder this time. I pulled my sweater, which had twisted around my body, back into place as I made my way blearily to the door.

There wasn't a peephole in the heavy wooden door, so I

opened it a crack with the chain on, expecting to see either Doug or the blond teenager.

"You've got the wrong room—" I broke off. The man, his hand raised to continue knocking, had light brown hair, chocolate brown eyes, and was sipping from a lidded to-go cup. The aroma of dark roast wafted through the gap.

"You're not Kate Sharp?"

"What? Who are you? How do you know my name?"

He stepped forward, his free hand extended.

Reflexively, I closed the door, cutting off whatever he was saying.

I leaned into the doorframe. "What's your name?"

"Alex. Alex Norcutt." He raised his voice, and his words carried through the door. "You sent me a text." His tone rose on the last words questioningly.

I hurried over to the bed, where I found my phone under several pillows. The screen informed me I had several unread text messages, all from Alex Norcutt. Grimacing, I scrolled through them. Yes, he was in town and could meet me in the morning. *How about nine?* After a gap of an hour, he texted again, *Nine still good to meet?* And, lastly, about an hour earlier he'd texted, *Stopping by the inn to see if you still want to meet.*

I went back to the door, unhooked the chain, and opened it. "Sorry. I'm still on L.A. time." There really had been no call to slam the door in his face. He wasn't threatening at all. He wore a denim shirt untucked over a white T-shirt with a pair of jeans. A worn leather jacket, combat boots, and a backpack slung casually over one shoulder completed his look, which was classic film crew casual. I would have recognized it, if I hadn't been so groggy.

He shrugged his shoulder slightly as he reached down to the floor to keep the backpack from slipping forward. "I thought you might be." He picked up a second cup that had been by his foot. "It's French Vanilla. That's about as fancy as we get coffee-wise here in Nether Woodsmoor." He was clean-shaven and his hair was slightly damp. I opened the door wider and caught a whiff of a clean soapy scent as he moved into the room.

"Thanks, that's wonderful." I took a sip and closed the door behind him. I pointed to the floor. "Watch out for the suitcase." Crossing to the window, I pulled the curtains back, flooding the room with light.

He paused, taking in the disarray of clothing spilling out of the bags scattered across the floor. "I see you're an aficionado of the Kevin Dunn school of organization."

"Ah, no. Actually, I'm a neat freak."

He raised an eyebrow.

"Really. I am. I drive people crazy." I wrinkled my nose. "If things are put away, I feel better."

"So this room must be making you insane."

"Now that I'm awake, it is." I took another sip of the coffee and finger combed my hair out of my face. "Sorry about the mess. I was looking—" I stopped abruptly. Did I want to tell him about Kevin? I ran a critical eye over Alex. He waited for me to continue with an easy, relaxed posture, his open gaze resting attentively on me.

"Can you give me about ten minutes? I'm glad you stopped by. I want to talk to you, but I'd like to get cleaned up. Can I buy you breakfast?"

"Sure. I'll wait for you downstairs."

I shut the door behind him, then grabbed some clothes and dashed into the bathroom where I gave myself half a second to check my reflection. Yep, it was as bad as I'd imagined. My eyeliner had smudged, giving me raccoon eyes, and my hair, except for being dark brown, had a definite Einstein-esque quality as it stood out around my head. I turned to the claw-footed tub that had been converted to a shower with a curtain on a circular rod overhead. The showerhead was attached to flexible metal tubing and had a mind of its own.

I conquered the showerhead, then pulled on jeans and a lightweight white sweater. I shoved my feet into flats as I combed my hair. It was still damp, but it would dry straight—it always did, no matter what the weather conditions were or what hairstyling jujitsu I applied—so I left it as it was and took a few minutes to add a little makeup. After shoving Kevin's clothes back in his suitcase and aligning it with the go-bag against the wall near my suitcase, I felt better. By the time I finished the last of the coffee and slid into a chair across from Alex in the inn's breakfast area, I felt almost human again.

"Impressive," Alex said.

"I hope the transformation wasn't that amazing."

"No, I meant it's impressive that it really did only take you ten minutes. I expected to be down here for at least an hour."

"There's only so much damage control a girl can do."

"You look great. Heck, you looked great up there, groggy and confused." He said the words casually, but his focused concentration was on me again, and I felt a blush heat my cheeks. He held his body in a relaxed, lounging posture, but there was an alertness in his gaze that reminded me of the big cats at the San Diego Wild Animal Park, the way they draped over branches, their bodies loose, but their eyes sharply observant.

"Right. With my matted hair and drool on my chin," I said, feeling more flustered for some reason.

"Self-deprecation is a habit with you, is it? You were charmingly rumpled."

"That's a very nice way of saying I was a bit on the scruffy side, but thank you for the compliment." Inwardly, I cringed. My voice sounded too formal, prissy even. Alex's eyebrows flared slightly, and he leaned back a bit.

"Sorry," I said. "I don't mean to be rude. I'm a bit...out of sorts."

"Hey, no problem," he said easily. "I was just trying to say you have that Audrey Hepburn thing going on. You know, you look classy no matter what. I've made you uncomfortable again. Sorry. I'm not trying to hit on you. I'm a photographer. I notice these things."

"Oh. Well, thanks."

The waiter arrived, the blond teen from the day before, and I tried to fight down the feeling that I'd been rude as I opted for a continental breakfast while Alex ordered a full English breakfast.

The menus were removed, and Alex crossed his arms on the table. "Now. What can I help you with?"

"Why don't you bring me up to date with what's happened here? How did it go?"

"Great. We got the Meryton and Rosings Park scenes sorted right away. We're using the historic center of a town called Buntley for the Meryton street scenes and the assembly room. There's a rather garish mansion up toward Sheffield—Cortland Hall—that has a pretentious vibe, which fitted perfectly for Rosings. Mr. O'Leery is keen to stay as close to the book as possible."

"Yes, that would be exactly right for Rosings Park. Austen describes Pemberley as having less splendor but more elegance than Rosings."

"Ah, yes. Mr. Dunn said you were the literary scholar and Austen expert."

"Not a scholar and certainly not an Austen expert."

"Well, you'll know more than me. I've only read one of her books."

"*Pride and Prejudice?*"

"Of course. I had to read it in school, and I'm afraid I took nothing away from it except that I enjoyed Mrs. Bennet. I reread it for this assignment."

"And what did you think of it on your second reading?"

"On the whole, I liked it. My last project had a reincarnation of Mr. Collins on the crew." He mock shuddered. "I admire the way Austen captured personalities."

"I think that's one reason she's still popular. Her characters are so lifelike. Austen wrote about people, flaws and strengths and all. And her characters grow and change through the books."

"Self-realization, you mean? Yes, I can see that with Elizabeth and Darcy, too. Of course, speaking as a guy, *P & P* could have had more explosions and car chases or something like that...the Regency equivalent would be what? A curricle race? Although, I don't know what a curricle is. I think the production manager mentioned them."

"It was the Ferrari of the day, a light, fast chaise—or carriage—with two wheels. Young men showed off their horses and driving skills with them. If you want more drama, you should read Austen's juvenilia."

"Juvenilia?"

"Stories and plays she wrote in her teens to entertain her family. Plenty of beheadings, biting off fingers, attempted murder. Right up your alley."

"See, you are an expert. You know what juvenilia is *and* you know that Austen wrote some."

"Not really. I do love Austen. I will admit that. And I have picked up some period details. Anyway...what about the other locations?"

"Right. Second day, I showed them possibilities for Netherfield, Longbourn, and Pemberley. For the Netherfield exteriors, Mr. O'Leary liked a country home not too far from here called Drayton Park. The choice for Pemberley is even closer, Parkview Hall. It's just up the road, and we think it can do double duty for some of the Netherfield interiors as well. And that left Longbourn. Why don't we have Kevin join us for the details on the last choice? It's a bit tricky. He's around, right?"

"You've seen him?"

"No, not for a few days, but those were his bags upstairs."

I'd planned to be vague about Kevin and get as much information out of Alex as I could without giving anything away, but I abruptly reversed my plan. For one thing, Alex was technically working for us, for Premier Locations. He'd want to keep the project moving along and squash any rumors as much as Marci and I did. Another reason was that Alex was observant. There was something about his piercing gaze that told me it would be hard to put one over on him. Better to get him on my side than have him resent me later for holding back information.

I mirrored his posture, crossing my arms and leaning on the table. "Kevin is missing."

CHAPTER 4

$\mathcal{A}$LEX'S FOREHEAD WRINKLED INTO A frown. "Missing? I'm not sure I understand."

I blew out a sigh. "I don't either. Kevin isn't in L.A. His return ticket is still open. His rental car hasn't been returned." I glanced at the ceiling. "Kevin's bags are in my room because he never picked them up after he checked out. The inn has been storing them."

Alex put his coffee cup down slowly. His look of puzzlement had changed to concern. "I assume you've tried to reach him? Not answering his phone?"

"No. Marci—she's the office manager—has been trying to reach him since Monday. That's why I'm here."

"And you haven't called the police?"

I swallowed, wishing I'd thought out how much to tell him and how much to keep back. Our breakfast arrived, and I waited until the server left before I continued. "No. Kevin has some issues. Drinking issues." I raised my eyebrows, and Alex nodded slowly. He got it. I leaned closer. "I'm telling you this in confidence. It's not something that is generally known about Kevin. He's always managed to...keep it under control. Well, mostly. I only know because I was his assistant. He slipped up once, missed an important meeting. I went to check on him. If I hadn't done that, I probably never would have known."

"And it's important that it be kept quiet," Alex said. "The project with Mr. O'Leery and all." His tone wasn't snide or accusing. He was matter-of-fact. He understood the industry.

"Yes," I said with relief. "That's it exactly. I honestly thought I'd get here, find Kevin boozing it up in a local pub, sober him up, and hustle him home. But he's not here, not in Nether Woodsmoor."

"No, he's not." Alex looked up from cutting his tomatoes and caught the puzzled expression on my face. "I live in a cottage not too far from here." He pointed with his knife. "Just up the road. It's a small village. Word would get around if he was still here."

"Really." I popped a bite of a scone in my mouth.

"Oh yes. Los Angeles this isn't. No anonymity here. Whole village probably knows by now that you checked in and are asking about him." I sat back, shoulders slumping. He noticed. "But you don't have to worry. I put out the word before Mr. Dunn and his group arrived that we needed to keep it quiet about the project. They won't go blabbing it around."

"And you think that will work?"

"When it is a matter of money, people here can be quite closemouthed."

"Money? From the film, you mean?"

He went to work cutting some sort of fried sausage thing on his plate, nodding. "Yes. Nether Woodsmoor needs the economic shot in the arm that a film would bring, not to mention the follow-up tourism that could materialize if it is a hit. I made it clear that movie people value privacy and that discretion would give Nether Woodsmoor an edge." He lowered his voice. "Between you and me, Nether Woodsmoor is already at the top of the list. The houses around here have the look that Mr. O'Leery wants. Not a lot of hotel rooms in Nether Woodsmoor itself, I'll grant you that, but there is a resort in Upper Benning with plenty of hotel rooms for the crew, conference rooms for meetings, and ten private cottages for the star cast members. It's less than a twenty-minute drive. Knowing that the village would close ranks around the film people, help them out, that was icing on the cake for Mr. O'Leery."

I dusted the crumbs from my fingers and sat back, studying Alex's face.

"Do I have something stuck in my teeth?" he asked warily.

"No. It's just—and I blame it on the jetlag that I'm only now noticing this—but you don't sound British."

"What do I sound like?"

"I don't know," I said slowly. He didn't have the clipped, crisp British accent, but he didn't sound American or European either. "You don't sound like you're from anywhere, actually."

"Got it in one. Air force brat. I'm from everywhere and nowhere. Grew-up following my dad all over the States and then the world. He went on to diplomatic service, which to me and my sister, meant more of the same, still moving but less military bases."

"But you live here now? In Nether Woodsmoor?"

"Yes. That surprise you?"

"I assumed you were based in London or Manchester or somewhere like that."

"London is flooded with location scouts. I have the place to myself out here. Sole location scout. And it really is a great area with plenty to offer. Nether Woodsmoor is quintessentially English. Got the cottages with glorious flower gardens, rolling fields with hedgerows, drystone walls, and charming village complete with historic church and village green. I can see that you think I'm only taking it easy on myself, recommending my own village, but as I mentioned earlier, we have candidates for

Pemberley, Netherfield, and Longbourn. We had to go farther afield for Rosings Park and Meryton, but all within a manageable distance. And all new locations."

"Sounds promising." One of the challenges with doing the *Pride and Prejudice* film was that audiences already had locations and looks fixed in their collective mind because of the popularity of the BBC miniseries and the more recent feature film. The new film needed fresh locations, but ones that would be in keeping with the story.

"So Kevin and Mr. O'Leery liked what you showed them here?"

Alex nodded. "Yes, the whole group did. They made a short list before they left—well, before Mr. O'Leery left. I've been working the contracts and the permits for the top choices."

"Did Kevin mention anything new he wanted to show Mr. O'Leery? Perhaps something Kevin saw that Mr. O'Leery missed?"

"No. We all looked at everything together. Why?"

"Mr. O'Leery has been in touch with our office. He wants to see the 'new stuff' that Kevin promised him. Do you know what he's talking about?"

"No idea."

I sighed, thinking of the most important thing that was missing from Kevin's things upstairs, his camera. Was the 'new stuff' on his camera? I shifted in my seat and refocused on my main goal—finding Kevin. Hopefully when I found Kevin, I'd find his camera and the 'new stuff' as well. "So when was the last time you saw Kevin?"

"I feel like I'm in an episode of *Masterpiece Mystery.*" Alex grinned before he turned serious. "Thursday, late afternoon." He glanced at a table on the other side of the room. "We sat there by the window and roughed out a list of top choices."

"And then what happened?"

Alex shrugged as he put his napkin by his plate. "I shook hands with everyone and left."

"That's it? That's all you can tell me?"

"I had the impression that they weren't traveling to the airport together." At that moment, the blond teen arrived and stacked our plates.

"Henry," Alex said, "those two Americans who were here last week..." I widened my eyes, attempting to telegraph that I didn't want him to continue, but Alex went on. "Were you on the desk when they left?"

"Half the group checked out Friday morning, early. Mr. O'Leery checked out later that morning." Henry glanced at me quickly, obviously already up to speed on my connection to Kevin. "I wasn't there when Mr. Dunn left."

"But did you talk to him that afternoon? See him go out?"

"Oh, yes. After Mr. O'Leery left, Mr. Dunn was in the lobby. I asked if he needed anything, and he said he was only nipping out to the pub to meet a mate."

"Looks like talking to Louise is our next step," Alex said as Henry departed with our plates.

I pushed back my chair and stood. "I don't think that's a good idea."

"Hang on a minute," Alex said.

I turned back and saw him divert to speak to a woman seated at a table by the windows. As Alex approached, she reluctantly drew her gaze away from the newspaper propped between the teapot and her plate. Her face hardened into a glare at the sight of Alex, and he must have aborted any idea of having a conversation with her because he simply said, "Good to see you, Ms. Wallings," and rejoined me on the way to the door.

"Close friend of yours?"

"You could tell, could you?"

"I could tell how much she wanted you to stay away."

"Yes, that sums up my relationship with Eve Wallings. She just wants me to go away."

"Let me guess, she has a nice property?"

He groaned. "Amazing. Well, it's her uncle's, but he's elderly. She's the power behind the throne, so to speak. She makes all the decisions, and she's decided I'm to be avoided, but that is a battle for another day." We had crossed the lobby and were at the foot of the stairs, which were opposite the main door. "To the pub?" Alex asked.

I moved to the stairs. "We can't drop questions about Kevin and not expect the word to get out that something is wrong. I don't care how tight-lipped you think the village is here, word will get out."

He draped an arm over the newel post. "What other choice do we have?"

"We?"

"Well, you came to me for help. I have the morning free." He shrugged one shoulder. "I thought I'd hang with you, help you track down the missing Mr. Dunn."

As he said the last words, Doug came down the stairs, nodded at us, then continued on into the restaurant.

I closed my eyes for a second and blew out a calming breath. "Might as well put up a billboard on the village green," I muttered, climbing the stairs quickly.

Alex pounded up behind me. "No need. They all know already."

I continued down the hall to my room, and Alex kept up, only a pace behind me. "This isn't the big city. No secrets here. You might as well use that to your advantage."

I unlocked my door and paused before stepping inside. I put up a hand, palm out, in a gesture that was partly a warning and partly a 'back-off' gesture. "I appreciate your help, and I know you think everyone will keep quiet about Kevin, but I can't depend on that. You can't seriously expect me to believe that no one here is a gossip. This is about the survival of the company I work for, which employs three other people besides me. I don't want carelessness on my part to be the reason they are out of a job in a few weeks, okay?"

Alex studied my face, his dark eyes radiating concern. "I understand what you're saying. I want to find Mr. Dunn, too, you know. I have something at stake. Films set in the English countryside with directors like Mr. O'Leery are few and far between. I'll grant that there are a few people around here who find it hard not to pass on a bit of interesting news, but," he stepped closer and lowered his voice. His breath fanned over my cheek as he said, "I know who is trustworthy."

I was very aware of his face only inches from mine, and I realized that my breathing was doing funny things.

"Believe me," he continued, "I know who can keep things quiet. Louise Clement is one of the people you can trust." His tone was different. Was there a trace of bitterness or maybe wariness there? He stepped back before I could decide.

He switched to a playful, inviting tone as he waved his arm in a sweeping gesture. "So I leave it up to you. You're in charge. If you'd like to have me along, I'm yours for the morning." He placed his hand on his heart and bowed.

"Hmm...I bet you say that to all the girls—when you're trying to recruit their homes as a potential filming location."

"Only to the ones with a cozy cottage or stately manor."

"Okay. I know the value of someone with local knowledge, but we do it as quietly and as carefully as we can."

"Agreed."

"I've already talked to Louise. I asked her about Kevin—in a general way. I said I'd heard he was in the area and had she seen him? She said not since Friday."

"Did she say anything about the friend Henry mentioned?"

"No."

"Well, we know it wasn't Mr. O'Leery. He left that morning,

so it had to be someone else. Maybe Louise saw this other friend."

I looked at my watch. "Isn't it a little early?"

"No, it will be perfect. Louise will be there, getting ready and the door will be unlocked."

"You're sure?"

"That the door will be unlocked? That Louise won't gossip? Yes, to both."

I reluctantly said, "Okay, just let me get my coat." I didn't want to talk to Louise again, but unless I was going to visit pubs in an ever-widening circle, I didn't know what else to do.

Alex waited at the open door while I slipped on my coat. "You weren't kidding about being a neat freak, were you? You cleaned up before you came down to breakfast, didn't you?"

"Wouldn't you? It was a mess."

"It wasn't that bad."

I closed the door. We retraced our steps down the stairs and went outside, turning to walk along the path to the pub.

"I wish it had been like this when Mr. Dunn and Mr. O'Leery were here," Alex said as we walked. "First truly nice day we've had in a week."

The air was cool but clear and fluffy white clouds dotted the sky. Tiny green buds were visible on the tree limbs. "It wasn't this gorgeous?" I asked.

"No, gray and rainy off and on the whole time they were here."

"Don't worry. Kevin is able to see the potential no matter what the weather."

When we got to the pub, we both reached for the door. "Allow me." Alex pulled it open, then stepped back so I could go in first. I couldn't remember the last time a man had held a door open for me. Most guys I'd been out on dates with were usually so busy sending or receiving texts or phone calls that it was a wonder they didn't collide with the doors themselves.

The ambush date guy, the gamer, hadn't held the door open for me. In fact, I had serious doubts about whether he'd actually showered before the date.

I smiled at Alex as I stepped by him. I paused on the threshold, then spotted Louise at one of the chalkboards, writing the specials of the day in florescent yellow. I straightened my back and strode forward confidently. She saw Alex following me in and greeted him. "That bad of a day, is it? Need to start early?"

"No, just a question or two," Alex said. "We'd like to keep it between the three of us."

Louise nodded. I glanced around. A clatter of dishes sounded from the kitchen, but the area with the tables and behind the bar was empty. "I asked yesterday about a friend of mine, Kevin Dunn. You said he was in here Friday at lunch."

"Right."

"Did you happen to notice if he met someone?"

"Sure. He and Frank Revel sat by the fire, had a few pints. I kept an eye on them. At first it seemed friendly enough, but then they got a bit heated."

Alex looked at me, and I shrugged. "I've never heard of him."

Alex and Louise exchanged a look, then Alex said, "I know him slightly. I met him one night here at the pub."

Louise nodded a confirmation. "He's a regular. Comes in a couple of times a month."

"So what happened? Did they leave together?"

"No. They were having a go at one another. Just words, you understand, but I was about to send Phil over there to tell them to settle down when your friend stormed out. Frank followed him. That's the last I saw of them."

CHAPTER 5

"SO YOU KNOW THIS FRANK Revel?" I asked as we left the pub.

"In a way."

"What does that mean?"

"I know him professionally. He was a producer. Retired recently and moved to this area about a year ago. He lives in Upper Benning."

"You've been to his house?" I asked.

Alex held up his phone. The screen displayed a map. "No, but only one 'Frank Revel' shows up anywhere near here. Are you driving or am I?"

I wasn't anxious to navigate the roads again and even less anxious to do it with someone observing me. "You."

"My car's back at the inn."

We made the short walk back to the inn along the footpath. I almost changed my mind about driving when he opened the passenger door of a classic red two-seat convertible and a sheaf of paper slid out. He caught it before it hit the ground and walked around me to deposit it in the trunk. "Sorry. Been doing a bit of research."

The woman who'd given him the cold shoulder in the restaurant came into the parking lot. Small-framed and thin, she wore a mud-colored tweed coat with surprisingly stylish ankle boots embellished with buckles. The sun glinted on the silver threads in her black hair, which was short around her ears and neck, but a longer sweep of bangs brushed her forehead above dark eyes. Her gait was determined and purposeful. She moved through the parking lot as if she had a plane to catch. She gave Alex a sharp nod without actually making eye contact and moved to her car, a faded and rusty mint-green Range Rover. She climbed in and slammed the door, catching a portion of her coat in the door.

Alex trotted over and tapped on the window. She wound down the window. "I have told you not to bother me. If anyone comes on my property again, I'll call—"

Alex raised his hands, palms up. "It's your coat. You've shut it in the door."

She frowned down at her coat, then opened the door and rearranged the fabric so that it was inside the car. "Thank you," she said gruffly and cranked up the window. She turned the engine on and was moving almost before Alex had time to step back.

"You're lucky she didn't run over your toes," I said when he returned.

"Oh, she'll come around someday," Alex said easily. "At least, that's what I tell myself." He grinned. "I live in hope." He removed more stuff from the front seat of his car, this time a stack of books. While he was occupied positioning those in the trunk, I stepped in for a closer look. Bits of paper, Post-it notes I realized, dotted the dash.

"What kind of car is this?" I asked. The exterior lines were sleek and stylish.

"It's a 1976 MG Midget. Appropriately named, right? Not much space." Alex came back to the passenger side and removed handfuls of crumpled paper from the footwell. He picked up two narrow Sprite cans along with a wadded paper bag and added them to the bundle of trash he cradled in his arms. "It's not as bad as it looks." He dropped everything in the appropriate bin at a recycling point a few feet away and spoke over his shoulder. "There's nothing biodegradable in there, I promise. No decomposing pizza slices forgotten under the seat."

He came back to the car, plucked the sticky notes off the dash, gave the passenger seat a few swipes with his hand, and stepped back. "Go ahead. My car is my office, usually. I would have tidied up if I'd known you'd be riding with me." He left the door open and walked around to the driver's side.

"It's fine. No worries," I said, too cheerfully.

"Top up or down?"

"What?"

He looked at his phone, which he'd popped into a holder attached to the dash. "It's a lovely day. Should I put the top down? I can, now that all my papers are battened down. It's still on the brisk side, but we can't be too picky about our weather here. We have to snatch the good days when we can." He looked at me as if he expected me to say no.

"By southern California standards this would qualify as winter." The sky was vibrantly blue, and the sun was streaming down, picking out drops of water clinging to the moss on the dark gray stone walls. "Sure. Let's put the top down."

After he folded the top back, I slid into the seat and buckled up. He settled into the driver's seat. "On the surface, it looks like a mess." He pulled a sticky note off the gearshift and handed it to me. My name and phone number were written in neat block printing. "I've got a system, but I'm sure you are more organized than I am. You're probably the sort who carries those wet antibacterial wipes. I bet you a pint that you've got some in there." He pointed with his chin toward my feet as he accelerated onto the road. "Feel free to decontaminate everything, if it makes you feel better."

"No, I'd never..." I edged my purse to the farthest point in the footwell and checked to make sure it was closed.

The road cut through the countryside of open, gently rolling green fields divided by the stone walls and layered with occasional groves of trees. He leveled his gaze at me. "It's nothing to be ashamed of, you know," he said with mock seriousness. "Carrying antibacterial wipes. I bet you have hand gel cleaner stuff, too."

I wanted to be irritated with him, but found myself smiling instead. "Okay, it's true. I carry wipes and hand gel."

"Wonderful."

"Wonderful?"

"Yes. It means you're organized, orderly, neat. The kind of person who carries tissues and plasters and bug repellent. I bet you're always prepared. Nothing wrong with that." Alex shifted down, slowing the car to a crawl where a lane bisected the major road. He pointed down the lane. "That's Grove Cottage, the future Longbourn for the film."

The lane ran up a hill, then dipped down. The house was set in the hollow, so I had to stretch to get a glimpse of the pale yellow two-story stone building. I braced my arm on the door, inching higher, trying to see as much of the square Georgian-style home as I could. Front windows, four on each floor, flanked a central door under a medium pitched roof with a pair of chimneys on each end of the house. "You don't sound too excited."

"Don't I? Better work on that. Of course, Becca Ford is probably excited enough to make up for any lack of enthusiasm on my part." He merged back onto the main road.

"The owner?"

"Yes. One of those managing types who wants to be involved in every detail. I receive an average of four calls a week from her. Already had one from her yesterday. I talked her out of adding a circular portico over the front door so that it would look more like the house in the BBC miniseries version of *P & P*." He sighed. "She doesn't seem to understand we want it to look different. Mr. Dunn almost nixed it from the list before I took them to see anything because of the yellow stone being too similar to the ochre-colored Bennet house in the other production."

I nodded, knowing Alex would have given Kevin and Mr. O'Leery a preliminary overview of the locations they were going to see before actually visiting any properties.

"It will do fine, I'm sure," Alex said.

"But it wasn't your first choice, was it?" I asked.

He frowned. "You read me a little too well."

"I recognize that wistful tone, is all. You had something else in mind, didn't you?"

"Yes. Coventry House. Would have been perfect. Grove Cottage will work, but it will be tight—tighter than I'd like. The house is small and the land around it is quite limited."

"Space is important," I agreed. Not only did you have to figure out if the location itself was right for the production, you also had to take into account if the surrounding area could handle the influx of people and equipment that a shoot would bring. The area around the possible location wasn't the first thing to consider, but it was a critical factor. The crews that accompanied a production had to have room to work, not to mention proper electrical capacity as well as restrooms and trash disposal, all very non-glamorous items that added up to the success or failure of location shoots.

"Coventry House is bigger, but not too ostentatious for the Bennets. Plenty of area around the house to set up. Completely different look than Grove Cottage, too. No one would think our *P & P* is the same as one that's already been done. But it's Eve Wallings house."

"Oh, I see."

"She won't see me. You saw her reaction this morning. She flat out refused to take a call or open the gate at the end of their drive. She can stonewall like no one I've ever seen."

"You couldn't talk to the uncle?"

"No, Edwin Wallings is ninety-three. Eve is his niece or great-niece, or niece twice removed, something like that. She's related to him, anyhow. She moved into Coventry House several months ago after Mr. Wallings fell. She guards him like a Rottweiler, making sure nothing upsets him. Eve says he's too frail too even consider the possibility of a film crew on his property."

"Did you offer a temporary relocation to somewhere nice and warm, perhaps with nursing care for the uncle? It would be a bit of a vacation for her, too."

"I would have, if she'd talked to me. No, the best I could do was float the idea to her through her friend Beatrice." His hands relaxed on the wheel, and he smiled. "Now, Beatrice is a definite friend of the production. Astute, too. She's got Parkview Hall, our version of Pemberley, actually producing income. A tiny income, but to get any of these old piles to earn their keep, so to say, is an accomplishment. I'll show you Parkview Hall on the way back. Here's Upper Benning now."

I PUSHED the buzzer for the third time, leaving my finger on the white button for a full ten seconds, which doesn't sound like a long time, but listening to the drone of the bell on the other side of the front door was beginning to annoy even me. Frank Revel lived in a modern area. With its mix of angular duplex homes and three- and four-story apartment buildings crowded into a small patch of land, it was the antithesis of picturesque Nether Woodsmoor.

"I don't think he's home." Alex stood behind me, his combat boots sinking into the mushy strip of grass that ran between the sidewalk and the concrete slabs that marked the entrance of each home.

"I'm not giving up. This guy is the only lead I have. If we can't track him down, then I think my next stop either has to be the police or the local hospital." I stepped off the concrete, moved to the front door of the other half of the duplex, and leaned on its buzzer. Same result as the first time.

I walked back to stand beside Alex, hands braced on my hips as I surveyed the street. Location scouting is not for the timid. "Kevin always says the front door is the easiest to close. Or keep closed, in this case." I moved up the street until I found a muddy path that ran between the duplex buildings. I straightened my shoulders and moved down it, mentally bracing to be pushy, if I had to. Alex followed me.

The path opened onto a small alleyway behind the duplexes. I counted the homes until we were back to Frank Revel's house, then opened the gate and found a man kneeling beside a row of upturned earth. He levered himself up with a grunt and turned to me, a spade dangling from one hand. He was carrying plenty of extra pounds in his gut and didn't move quickly, but I stopped where I was. His expression under a fringe of gray hair was anything but welcoming. "Take yourself off. I don't want whatever you're selling."

"I'm not selling anything. I'm looking for Kevin Dunn."

From his bushy eyebrows to the tip of his chin, his face flushed, and his grip around the spade tightened. He muttered something that I didn't catch then said, "Out. Get off my property." He came toward me diagonally across the small garden, stepping carefully over the rows of turned earth.

Alex put a hand on my shoulder, and shifted in front of me. I dipped my shoulder and moved in front of him. "So Kevin isn't here?" I asked.

Frank Revel stopped a few feet away and gave out a bark of laughter. "Here? No, the scheming louse is not here." He focused on Alex. "You're Norcutt, from Nether Woodsmoor."

"Yes. Good to see you again, sir."

A roughly-framed shed stood beside the gate. Clear plastic covered half of it, creating a greenhouse. Frank Revel tossed the spade onto a bench positioned by the door to the shed and picked up a towel. "What's this about," he asked as he wiped his forehead.

The flush had faded to pink and since he wasn't holding the spade any longer, I stepped closer. "I'm Kate Sharp. I work for Kevin." I wished I could gloss over the truth, come up with some glib lie, but I knew looking into his hard face that it wouldn't work. "I don't know where Kevin is. As far as I can tell, no one has seen him since you were with him at the pub. Louise said you argued."

He rubbed the cloth over his face again and muttered a curse, his gaze fixed over my shoulder. "If that don't beat all," he finally said, switching his attention back to me. "That's vintage Kevin, all right." With a quick snap of his arm, he threw the towel down by the spade. "Managing to bring me trouble even when he's not around." The movement was so unexpectedly sharp and crisp, I tensed, ready to move backward, but he turned away, picked up a shovel that was propped against the shed, and walked down one of the garden rows. "I haven't seen him since Friday," he said over his shoulder. "We went our separate ways."

"Did he mention where he was going later that day?"

"No. Close that gate on your way out." He half turned and pointed the shovel at me. "If you can't find him, don't send any coppers around here."

～

I SLID INTO THE CAR, dropped my head onto the headrest, and blew out a breath.

Alex spun the steering wheel and pulled away from the curb. "Dealing with people isn't your thing, is it?"

I rolled my head and looked toward him. "That obvious, is it?"

He shrugged one shoulder. "You seemed to brace yourself before we went around the back. You know, shoulders back, hands clenched at your sides. And you got this fiercely determined look on your face. You did the same thing before we talked to Louise."

"I didn't realize it was that noticeable. It's not so much the confrontation bit—I don't mind that. I like getting things done. It's interacting with people. I know it's not my strong point. Give me a list of locations, a schedule, and a budget, and I'm your girl. Sweet-talking the homeowners, though, that's hard for me."

"Well, you got information out of Louise earlier."

"Oh, I can do it. I've learned. It's just not my favorite part of the job. After I started working with Kevin there was no way I was going back to manning the reception desk and listening to the whine of the dental drill all day. I love everything else about what I do—being out, seeing interesting places, researching possible locations, taking photos, hitting on that exactly right location, and working with the pre-production teams to slot all the locations into the best schedule possible. I'm getting better at the cold meet-and-greet as Kevin calls it. Maybe someday it will be a breeze for me. It is for Kevin. He can't wait to meet people. He can't imagine anyone not wanting to talk to him." I rolled my head back and looked out the window. "I hope his... enthusiasm...didn't get him in trouble. There have been a few times Kevin pushed too hard. The result wasn't good."

"So what's the history between Kevin and Frank Revel?"

"I have no idea, but I can ask Marci. She might know." I

found my cell phone in my bag, but stopped before I dialed. It was something like two or three in the morning. I couldn't call her now. I shoved the phone back in my bag. "Too early, though."

I propped my elbow up on the side of the door and watched the blurring shades of green swish by.

Alex raised his voice. "Want me to put the top up?" Clouds had filled the sky, and we were flying through the checkerboard of alternating spots of sunlight and shadow.

"No, it's fine." I blinked and brushed away some strands of hair that the wind whipped into my face. Earlier, while Alex gathered his sticky notes in a neat pile before putting the top down, I'd pulled my hair into a long braid. The buffeting wind had teased most of it loose.

"The local police officer wouldn't happen to be in your circle of acquaintances, would he?" I asked.

Alex glanced at me out of the corner of his eye. "Sure, I know Constable Albertson. I have to coordinate with the authorities occasionally for road closures. You're thinking of contacting him? Even after what Frank Revel said?"

"I don't have a choice. Not really. I can't think of anything else to do. Kevin isn't in Nether Woodsmoor, and I haven't been able to run him to ground in any of the surrounding pubs. He had a public argument with an old friend and hasn't been seen since. I think I better report it." I rubbed my hand across my face. "The last thing I want to do is go to the police, but what else can I do?"

Alex didn't answer, and it took me a few moments to realize we'd left the main road and were traveling down a smaller one. We entered a stretch of road where towering trees crowded close, their bare branches touching overhead, creating a long tunnel-like archway. Alex eased off the gas and downshifted as a gap in the trees approached. He slowed to a crawl, and let the car roll to a stop on a gravel turnout.

I reached for the door handle, ready to run, news stories about criminals who lured unsuspecting tourists to isolated spots flashing through my mind. Alex turned off the ignition and flung his hand out toward the windshield. "Now there's a location. Haven't been able to use it yet."

His voice was perfectly normal, and he wasn't even watching me. I looked in the direction he'd indicated. A bridge of golden stone crossed a wide sweep of a river. The bridge's three supporting arches reflected in the rippling water.

"It's gorgeous." I climbed out of the car, but not with the intention of running away, only to get a better view. It was a Grade-A Prime location. My fingers itched to get my camera and record the quiet beauty of it, but I'd left it in my room at the inn.

Alex moved around to the hood. I joined him there, leaning against the warm metal. Alex said, "This is the long way back to Nether Woodsmoor. It's further, but it's a nice drive. The road we were on swings wide then curves back and runs over the bridge, but this is the best view."

The air was cool enough that the heat from the car's engine felt good on the back of my legs. Overhead, the wind whispered through the tree limbs. The engine metal clicked and pinged.

"Kevin always says to bring the camera, that the time you don't have it, is when you'll want it the most."

"You've worked with him a long time?"

"Yeah, I was his assistant. I didn't know anything when he took me on. Nothing about aperture or permits or white balance."

I looked over at Alex. "How did you get into location scouting?"

"The roundabout way. I love snowboarding, skiing, mountain biking, anything to do with the outdoors. I filmed everything, lots of live-action material. I started posting my stuff on-line, then a buddy of mine created his own line of snowboards. He asked me to help him with the marketing. I created a YouTube video for him. It went viral and...well, after a bit, I realized I wasn't going to win any X-Game Championships, but I might be able to make a living with my camera."

"Do you still do that? Sports photography?"

"Some. Not too much demand for it around here. The sports stuff is the icing. Catalog shots are my bread-and-butter."

I was tempted to ask why he had tucked himself away in a sleepy English village if X-Game sports appealed to him the most, but he suddenly stood and paced to the edge of the clearing. "Best be getting on."

"Right." I stood and joined him at the point where the gravel thinned and a band of long grass marked a drop of several feet to the water. "Thanks for bringing me here. It's very peaceful." The whole time we'd been talking only one car had driven over the bridge. I could imagine horse-drawn carriages and coaches making their way over the bridge and ladies in long skirts and bonnets strolling along its length.

"I thought you'd like it." He kept his gaze on the bridge as he spoke.

"I did." I rolled my shoulders. "Okay, on to the police. You can drop me there if you need to get going..." My words trailed off. Alex's gaze had sharpened as he stared at the bridge.

"What is it?" I turned to look at the bridge. Clouds had been drifting across the sky, dappling the scene with shadow, but now the clouds blocking the sun were shifting, and the filtered light gradually transitioned to full sunlight. The bright sunshine sparkled on the surface of the water, glittering on the tiny ripples, but the clearer light also penetrated down below the surface, illuminating what had been opaque when the cloud covered the sun. "Is there something down there, underwater?" I asked.

"I think so." Alex went to the car, popped the trunk and returned with his camera, attaching a long lens as he walked. He put it to his face, then handed it to me. "It's a car." His voice sounded funny.

I looked through the viewfinder, and my heart dropped. "A black one."

CHAPTER 6

*A*NOTHER CLOUD SLID IN FRONT of the sun, and all I could see was the reflection of the bridge and the cloud-dotted sky. "Too cloudy." Automatically, I slipped the strap of the camera around my neck and set off down a path beside the water. "This way?" I called.

"Ah—yes, but I don't think you should..."

I pressed on down the path, the long wet grass soaking my jeans around my ankles, telling myself I had to be mistaken. The path wound away from the water, back into the dense stand of oaks. Running footsteps sounded behind me as Alex caught up, punching numbers into his phone as he half-walked, half-jogged. He pressed his phone to his ear.

The path rose, the trees fell away, and the bridge came into view. I scrambled up an incline, a mix of rocks and grass, and emerged onto a flat grassy area beside the road. The bridge was a few feet away. I closed the distance as the cloud glided away, and the water again became transparent. I shifted the camera, pulling it from my chest to my side as I leaned over the parapet. "It is. It really is a car," I whispered.

The car wasn't far underwater, probably only a foot or two,

but it was completely submerged. Under the shimmering surface, I could clearly see the shape of it and even make out a Mercedes logo on the hood. I swallowed hard. I stood there, the cold stone of the bridge pressing against my waist, distantly aware of Alex moving around me, checking his phone.

Alex's warm hand rested on my shoulder. "Kate, are you okay?"

I stared at the water as I spoke. "This is so terrible—so much worse than anything I imagined might have happened." I didn't want to think about Kevin trapped inside a sinking car, but I couldn't stop the images from popping into my mind. I pushed away from the parapet, the stone rough and cold on my palms, and walked a few paces away.

"How long has he been there? Since Friday?" I turned back to Alex. "You said this road is one way to get to Nether Woodsmoor. What if he left the pub, went for a drive...or went to try and patch things up with Frank, and on the way back..." I looked at the clearing and had to stop talking. Two flattened parallel tracks cut through the grass at the edge of the clearing and carved down the steep bank to the water.

"It's possible, but we don't even know for sure this is Mr. Dunn's car."

I just looked at him.

"We don't know," Alex repeated. "Right now we need to call the police. The mobile service out here is patchy." He held up his phone and moved around. "I can't get a signal. Do you have your phone on you?"

"No, it's back at the car. I'll go get it," I said, already moving back to the path.

"Wait." Alex caught my arm. "You probably won't have any bars either. No, we'd better go to Parkview Hall. It's just up the road a bit." Alex gestured at the far side of the bridge. "They can call the police from their landline. That will be quicker than going back to the car."

"One of us should stay here, I think." I looked at the water. *How could we not have seen the car the instant we looked at the bridge?* Now that I'd spotted it, it was all I could see. It was like looking at one of those hidden pictures. At first, you can't make anything out, but once you've picked out the image, that's all you can see. "I mean, if he's been down there for days and days…it doesn't seem right to go off and leave him. I'll wait. You go on." I didn't want to wait alone on the bridge, knowing that Kevin's body was only a few feet away underwater in the car. *Those last moments would have been terrible.*

Alex studied my face for a second. "I'll stay. Go across the bridge. The gates for Parkview Hall are on the right. Big and imposing. Pillars on each side topped with urns. You can't miss it. Find Beatrice Stone. She knows me. She'll take care of everything," he called because I was already moving across the bridge.

"Beatrice Stone," I repeated to myself as I cleared the end of the bridge and jogged up the road's slight incline. At the crest of the small hill was a sign for Parkview Hall with an arrow pointing at two massive wrought iron gates set in a wall made of the same golden stone as the bridge. The gates stood open. I hurried through them, hopped over a chain draped across three poles that blocked the road, then bypassed a small shuttered kiosk with lists of ticket prices and hours. The drive wound through a grove of oaks. Between the thick tree trunks, I could see a manor house of honey-colored stone with a set of divided stairs rising to massive double doors. It looked a long distance away.

"You! You there," a voice called. "We're not open."

I turned to my right and peered through the trees. A woman with sunglasses perched on her head marched toward me, an oversized boxy trench coat flapping around her legs while two white mop-like dogs circled her feet, their paths intertwining with each other's but never coming near the woman's yellow galoshes. She carried a furled umbrella and pointed it at me. "No photography." She pointed the umbrella at the gates. "Out you go."

I left the drive and sprinted toward her. The dogs charged at me, their shrill yaps filling the air. I skidded to a stop. The woman shouted commands at them, but the dogs didn't stop. I backpedaled, but they were on me before I could take more than a step. They planted their muddy paws on my jeans, tails wagging and ears perked between barks.

"Worthless creatures," the woman said, still advancing with the umbrella point refocused on me. "Down! Down! Some watchdogs. Might as well have a flock of birds for all the good you two do."

I ignored the dogs. "Beatrice Stone?"

She was close enough now that I didn't have to shout, which was good because suddenly I was winded and shaky. *Maybe this is what shock felt like?* I braced a hand against a tree trunk, as one of the dogs popped up and planted its paws on the back of my knee, almost causing me to have a seat.

She shook her head and said firmly, "Not open yet. Come back next weekend—"

"There's been an accident. At the bridge. A car underwater. Alex..." *What was Alex's last name?* I couldn't remember. I reached down to one of the dogs that was practically shredding my jeans, and rubbed its ear. It stopped barking. The other dog whined and shimmied in protest. "We need you to call the police. There's no cell service at the bridge."

The umbrella point dipped to the ground. "Alex Norcutt? Oh, you're one of the movie people." She took my elbow. "Come along then. We'll phone Constable Albertson from the house, and then I'll run you down there in the Range Rover. Ladybug! Cupcake! *Off*, I said." In an undertone she added, "Don't let your grandchildren name your pets. I didn't think it through. Rather embarrassing to shout those names at the top of my voice."

I let her flow of words wash over me, nodding occasionally, which seemed to be all the interaction she required. We'd been walking diagonally through the woods, so that when we emerged from the trees we were at the far right-hand side of the building. I had a quick impression of a second-floor portico lined with massive columns and rows of windows stretching out on each side of the house from the central block. In a disjointed part of my mind, I had the fleeting thought the grandly elegant building would be perfect for Pemberley.

Beatrice steered me around the right-hand wing of the house along a drive that curved away to outbuildings. She took me into a short barrel vaulted tunnel on the ground floor that opened into a courtyard. She opened a heavy door, and the dogs shot by us, whipped through a room with coats hanging on the walls. A wide array of sports equipment, shoes, and gardening tools were scattered around. We followed the dogs into a kitchen where Beatrice parked me at a long wooden table, told a man rinsing dishes in the sink to give me a cup of tea and departed, yelling over her shoulder that she had to make a call.

The man turned from the sink, took one look at me, and reached for the teapot. He wore a long white apron tied at the waist over a dress shirt, tie, and slacks. He set a teacup in front of me and pushed a bowl of sugar cubes toward me. "Milk?"

"This is fine. Thank you." Beatrice was somewhere down the hall. Her rapid, but indistinct words filtered into the kitchen. The hot liquid seared my lips.

The man studied me with his black eyes. "You're pale. It looks as if you need something a bit stronger than tea." He shuffled away, running a hand dotted with liver spots over his baldhead, as he considered the cabinets. "Brandy," he pronounced and set off toward the door that Beatrice had disappeared through.

"No, this is perfect. I don't need anything else. Sorry to barge in on you. There's been an accident at the bridge…" I broke off.

He nodded. "Bit of a curve there. Takes some people unexpectedly. Especially the Americans." He turned his gaze to the window. "Should have a sign made." He nodded again. "Beatrice will see to it."

Beatrice burst into the room. "The constable is on the way. Alex must have flagged down a driver who had good mobile reception. Oh good, you had some tea. Plenty of sugar in it, I hope. Helps with the shock." She patted her pockets. "Glasses. Glasses."

"On your head, my dear," the man said. "There should be a sign leading up to the bridge."

"You're absolutely right, Harold." She settled her glasses on her nose. "Excellent idea. I'll bring it up with Constable Albertson."

I finished the tea and stood. "Ready."

"You met my husband, Harold?"

"Not formally, no, but he makes an excellent cup of tea." I stepped forward. "I'm Kate Sharp."

He inclined his head. "Delighted."

His manner was old world chivalry, and for a moment I felt I should curtsy or something, but then Beatrice plucked a set of keys off a row of hooks on the wall. The dogs skidded back into the kitchen and ran in a circuit between our feet and the door. "No, you bothersome things, you can't go." She turned to Harold. "Are you coming along, too?"

He shook his head. "Things to do here," he said vaguely, gesturing to the sink.

After deftly closing the yapping dogs in the kitchen, Beatrice led the way out of the house to a mud-splattered Range

Rover parked near a building I assumed was once the stables. It was the same type of car that Eve Wallings had been driving, but this one looked even older and more beat-up than hers. I climbed in, and Beatrice hit the gas. We bumped over the lane that led around the house to the tree-lined drive. "Won't take long," she said as I gripped the door panel with one hand and fastened my seatbelt with the other.

Rows of trees whipped by, and then she swung wide around the chain, blocking the end of the drive and we were through the gates. She parked at the end of the bridge, probably on ground that was part of Parkview Hall's land. I slammed the door and hurried over the bridge to a scene completely different from the one I'd left.

A tow truck was lumbering into a position in the clearing where the tracks cut down the bank. Farther up the road, a police car angled across the road. A knot of people stood at the end of the bridge, including a man in a police uniform. I spotted Alex standing alone on higher ground on the far side of the tow truck. As I reached the end of the bridge, the man in uniform—the constable, I guessed—stepped away from the small group and approached, glancing beyond me to the Range Rover and Beatrice, who was moving slower than I was and hadn't crossed the bridge yet. He consulted a notepad. "You're Kate Sharp?" I nodded. "You think you knew the driver?"

I blew out a breath. My thoughts skittered to Marci. I'd have to call her. Secrecy was now at the bottom of my list of important things. "Yes. My boss, Kevin Dunn. I've been trying to find him. He didn't return from a business trip." I looked toward the tow truck where a man in waders had hopped down from the cab and was working on a pair of gloves. "I thought he'd still be in the area, but I haven't been able to find him. I had just decided that I needed to call the police. Then we spotted the car…"

The constable's craggy face had a sympathetic expression as he looked up from the notepad. "Missing, was he?"

"Yes, since Friday."

The constable glanced at Alex, who'd joined us. "You said 'we.' That would be the two of you?" He moved his pencil point from Alex to me.

"Yes." I pointed across the water to the outcropping of land where Alex's red car still sat. "We were over there, looking at the view when the light changed."

The constable looked up from his notebook. "The light changed? How?"

"The reflection of the clouds masked what was under the surface. The sun came out and then…we saw the car."

The man in waders shouted for the constable then turned back and made a circling motion with his hand to another man in coveralls. The constable said, "I'll have more questions for you in a moment." He moved to the group gathered at the edge of the bank. A deep mechanical whir filled the air. I slowly crossed the bridge.

Alex said, "Do you want to wait in my car? You don't have to be here. I'll tell Constable Albertson where you are."

"No, I think I should be here. I don't want to be, but it seems like it would be wrong somehow to go hide in the car."

Stretched taut, the cables slowly dragged the Mercedes out of the water. The trunk appeared first, water sluicing across the smooth surface, then the back doors emerged. Beatrice came to stand on the other side of me.

The front doors and windshield cleared the water next, the sunlight catching the surface of the windshield and reflecting directly in my eyes. I put a hand up, but the tow truck continued to pull the car out of the water, causing the angle of the windshield to change, and the reflection vanished. I squinted, bracing myself, expecting to see Kevin pinned to the front seat by the seatbelt, but the front seat was empty.

A buzz went up from the small group gathered around the car. It was fully out of the water now, but still dangling at an almost ninety-degree angle down the steep riverbank, water pouring from the seams of the doorframes and the hood.

I'd been gripping the stone of the bridge, but now I pushed away and took several steps toward the car. The cables continued to reel the car in, inching it up until it was on level ground. One of the men broke away from the group and opened both the front and back doors on one side, stepping quickly away as water cascaded out along with bits of paper.

I'd been walking toward the car, but stopped. It was empty.

CHAPTER 7

"EMPTY. COMPLETELY EMPTY," I SAID to no one in particular. Seeing the car underwater had been awful and my mind had immediately gone to the worst possibility—that Kevin, either through his own negligence or because of some accident, had run off the road, been trapped inside and drowned, but now that his body wasn't in the car...I didn't know what to think.

Beatrice pushed another cup of tea across the table to me. We were back in her kitchen, Alex and I. I hadn't seen Harold since we'd returned, but then again, I hadn't really been paying that much attention. The last half hour or so was a bit foggy.

"It could be a good sign," Alex said.

I set my teacup down in its saucer with a click. "You mean, that if he was in the car when it went over the edge, he got out before it was completely submerged?"

"Yes."

"The same thought crossed my mind. But if that happened, wouldn't a door have been open? Or the window rolled down?"

"There is that," Alex admitted, sending me a faint smile. "Trying to look on the positive side here."

"Or, he might not have been in it at all," Beatrice said, as she sat down with us at the table with her own cup of tea. "Perhaps his car was stolen."

"Then where *is* Kevin? Why hasn't he checked in with Marci? She's our office manager back in California," I explained to Beatrice. "Or why hasn't he shown up at the inn?"

There was a long moment of silence filled only with the clink of Beatrice's spoon as she stirred her tea.

A knock sounded, and Beatrice went to answer it. Constable Albertson followed her back into the kitchen, refusing a cup of tea as he took a seat beside me.

"I'm sorry to have to tell you, but we've found him," he said.

I could tell from his demeanor and tone the news wasn't good. "Where?" I asked, my stomach clenching.

"He was downstream—quite far actually—about halfway between the bridge and Nether Woodsmoor. Deserted section of the river, not much out that way. None of these new housing developments with people walking their dogs. I figure that's why he wasn't spotted straight away. Looks as if he got out of the car before it went under, but got swept away in the tide. He was caught under the roots of an old tree trunk."

"But the water, it was so calm," I protested, thinking of how bulky and strong Kevin was. Perhaps an ocean swell might overpower him, but not that smooth-flowing river.

"Today it is, but we've had several storms. If he went in right after one of those...well, the rivers swell up and can be quite fast moving," Constable Albertson said.

I looked to Alex, who nodded his head in confirmation. Beatrice stood, propped up against a wooden dresser with china and dishware ranged along the upper shelves, a sad expression on her face. "It's true. I've lived here for over thirty years and the river does rise with the rains, sometimes in a rather frightening way. Quite dangerous."

Constable Albertson said to me, "If you could come with me, we need to take care of a few things at the station."

"Of course." I pushed away from the table. The questions could wait. Certain things had to be done. All that really mattered now was that Kevin was dead.

~

THE NEXT MORNING, I awoke after a restless night. There was no confusion about where I was this morning, and I had none of the lingering grogginess of jetlag, despite not having slept well. Thoughts of Kevin, questions about what had happened to him, the future of Premier Locations, and even how to handle getting Kevin's body back to California had filled many hours of the night. I'd asked some of the questions yesterday, but hadn't gotten any real answers about anything yet, not even when Kevin's body would be released. At least I'd been able to get in touch with Marci and break the news to her myself. That had been the worst, telling her what had happened. I checked my phone, but didn't have any messages. She had said she would get in touch with me after she told the girls at the office. She also had to talk to Mr. O'Leery as well as look for contact information for Kevin's relatives.

I stared at the ceiling, still feeling a bit numb, thinking how badly everything had turned out. I'd expected the trip to have some difficult points, but finding out your employer had died was so far from simply sobering someone up and getting them home.

The events of yesterday had a momentum of their own. Once Kevin's body had been discovered, I'd been swept up and was being pulled along in the wake created by the wave of activities around his death. *Nothing to do now, but get through it.* I pushed back the covers and dragged myself to the shower.

Later, as I came down the stairs, Doug looked up from the

front desk and tilted his head toward the breakfast area. "Someone waiting for you."

I turned the corner, expecting to see Alex, but the room was empty except for a slight man with a narrow face seated at a table with a to-go cup of coffee and a cell phone in front of him. Everything about him was brown from his wavy hair to his pale brown suit down to his polished dress shoes. He'd been absorbed in his phone, but when I entered, he put the phone down and stood. "Kate Sharp? Detective Chief Inspector Quimby. Do you have a few moments?"

"Yes, of course."

He gestured at the seat across from him, and I sat down with a bump. *Detective Chief Inspector?* Quimby pressed his brown tie to his chest as he sat down.

Henry arrived, pushing his swath of blond hair off his forehead. "Like to try the English breakfast today?" he asked.

"Go ahead. I've already breakfasted," Quimby said.

"Just coffee for me now." If I was going to be interviewed by a detective, there was no way I was doing it over greasy breakfast meat. "So you must be here about Kevin. Is this normal with an accident? That seems a little…" The word *overkill* came to mind, but I wasn't about to say that word out loud.

Henry returned with my mug of coffee, and Quimby waited until he left before saying, "Mr. Dunn's death wasn't an accident."

I was lifting my mug to my lips, but I put it back down. "What do you mean?"

"I can't go into specifics. All I can say is that he didn't lose control and run off the road." The only bit of color about Quimby was his pale green eyes, which stood out against the palette of brown. He narrowed his eyes as he studied me. "But you already knew that, didn't you?"

"No, I didn't. Know it, I mean. It was only that there were some things that seemed odd—not right."

Quimby's phone chimed. He glanced at it, then said, "What things?"

"Well, when they towed the car out of the water, it was empty, but all the doors and windows were closed. If Kevin had driven off the road and managed to escape, wouldn't there have to be an open door or window?"

Quimby nodded. "Anything else?"

I twisted my mug around, but didn't pick it up. "And where had he been? Why hadn't he checked in with us? He was here scouting locations for a new *Pride and Prejudice* film."

His phone chimed again, and after a quick check, he looked back to me. "Let's rewind, go over a few things." He tapped the screen on his phone. "The local constabulary has given me your details. You've been employed with Mr. Dunn's company, Premier Locations, for three years?" I nodded, and he went on, reciting my résumé. "First as his assistant for a year and a half, then promoted to the position of location scout for his company for the last year and a half?"

"That's right."

"What did you do before that?" he asked, his tone indicating genuine curiosity. It was a question I got a lot—location scouting is an unusual job, and people are curious about how someone gets into the field.

"I had a—um, I think over here you call it a gap year." He nodded, and I went on. "It wasn't planned. I was in grad school, getting my doctorate, but there were difficulties." I paused. Odd, how a family falling apart could be described in a few words. "I wasn't able to go back to grad school. I worked as a temp for about a year, then I heard about the opening for Kevin's assistant."

"I see." Quimby refocused on his phone. "And Mr. Dunn arrived here last week to look for locations for a new film, but he didn't return to California on Friday. You arrived on Tuesday of this week." I confirmed that he had the dates right.

Quimby put his phone down, sat back, and crossed his arms. "I must ask, why didn't you contact the police? By the time you arrived, he'd been missing four days."

I paused, blew out a breath. "Sorry. It's just awful—the whole thing—knowing that Kevin was in the river…" I rubbed my forehead, deciding that complete honesty about my trip was the only way to go. Anything else would be foolish. They would find out the truth about Kevin soon enough. "Kevin was a recovering alcoholic. He'd had a few…incidents when he slipped up. We—the office manager and I—thought that was what had happened. We didn't want to do anything to endanger the *P & P* film job. Rumors can be the death of you in the film business. If word got out that Kevin had bailed…well, it could mean we'd lose the project."

"Which, I presume, would be a good bit of income for your company."

"Yes."

"So keeping the job was critical."

I leaned back, glad he understood. "Yes. That's it, exactly. I thought I'd find Kevin either drunk or sleeping it off somewhere around this village or in a pub not too far away."

"And when you didn't find him right away, why didn't you contact us?"

"I had decided to do that when Alex and I spotted the car."

Quimby's eyebrows shot up. "Really? You'd decided *moments* before?"

"Well, not moments. It was after we talked to Frank Revel."

Quimby touched his phone screen again. "Ah, yes. His friend, the one he argued with at the pub."

"Yes, Frank was my last idea. Louise at the pub told us they'd met. I thought Frank Revel might know where Kevin was. Or Kevin might be at his house. He wasn't. I didn't know what else to do, and I was worried that something bad had happened."

He stared at me for a long moment, his face expressionless. My heart began to thud. *He doesn't believe me.*

Finally, he said, "When was the last time you were in contact with Mr. Dunn?" I realized I'd curled my hands into fists and relaxed my fingers.

"Me, personally? Um, that would have been last week sometime. I'm not sure what day. Before he left, definitely. Monday, I guess. I think he—yes, he was in the office that day." Suddenly my nervousness was obvious. I couldn't put together a couple of coherent sentences.

"And did you have any contact with him once you arrived here?"

"No—how could I? He was missing."

Quimby flared a single eyebrow, indicated his skepticism as clearly as if he'd spoken aloud. "You say you spent the day with Alex Norcutt. How long ago did you meet him?"

"Yesterday."

"Hmm," Quimby murmured, transmitting a we'll-see-about-that vibe. "What will happen to Premier Locations?"

I shrugged. "I don't know. It depends on...well, many things. Worse case scenario would be that it will close." Normally, the thought of losing my job would induce gnawing worry and cold sweats about bills and groceries, but it didn't seem so important compared with the fact that Kevin was dead.

"But you and your fellow employees could continue on? Perhaps under a new name? You have the experience, the contacts, to form your own company?"

"Yes, I suppose that's true, but I don't know that will happen. I don't really want to own a business, and I can't imagine that either Marci or Zara would either."

"Nevertheless, it is a possibility. Do you have any idea about Mr. Dunn's will?"

"No, of course not. I don't even know if he had one. Why would you think I'd know something like that?"

Quimby shrugged. "Office relationships happen. You worked with Mr. Dunn. Were you ever involved with him?"

"With Kevin? No…that's…that's—" I broke off. "He was over twenty years older than me."

"You find the idea distasteful?"

"I find the question distasteful." I was nervous about where his questions were going, but I couldn't let the insinuation pass. "Kevin was like a dad to me. He taught me the business and helped me whenever he could. He did that for everyone in the office."

"So he had no enemies?"

We'd switched tracks so quickly that I felt slightly thrown off. "What? No."

"No one who disliked him? What about Frank Revel?"

I blew out a breath, thinking that if Quimby was trying to rattle me, he was very good at his job. "I don't know what Kevin and Frank's history was. As far as anyone else…well, the movie business is cutthroat, but isn't that how it is in every business? Sure, there are people who aren't—or weren't—fans of Kevin, but can I think of anyone who'd want to hurt him? No."

Quimby flicked his thumb on the screen of his phone. "Do you smoke, Ms. Sharp?"

"No."

"Do you own a brown Burberry trench coat?"

"No. Burberry is a little beyond my reach."

He scrolled through more data on his phone.

"What was your arrival flight number?"

I found the info in my Moleskine notebook, and he tapped it into the phone. My palms felt sweaty. In fact, I felt clammy all over. *Get a grip*, I told myself. Just because he was checking my movements didn't mean anything. It was probably standard procedure. He asked more about my activities, and I summarized what I'd done from the moment my plane landed until I returned to the inn last night after answering the constable's questions.

I pressed my hands down on my jeans and leaned forward over the table. "I'm trying to help you, but I get the feeling that I might need a lawyer. I wasn't even in the country until two days ago. Surely I'm not a suspect."

Quimby pocketed his phone and stood, his smile bland. "Oh, I suspect everyone."

~

I SAT THERE, stunned, after Quimby left, staring at the business card he'd placed on the table as he told me to get in touch if I thought of anything else that might be helpful to the investigation. I picked up my cell phone and swiped the card from the table. I'd been so thrown off by Quimby's questions that I had completely forgotten to ask any questions of my own. I dialed and was surprised when Quimby answered immediately. I identified myself, and he said, "You thought of something else so soon?"

"No, I realized I didn't get the details from you—" my voice caught, and I had to clear my throat. "On when Kevin's body would be released."

"It won't be immediately. There are...examinations that have to be made. You'll be informed when you can make arrangements. I'm sorry, but that's the best answer I can give you now. Please keep me informed of your movements."

"Movements?"

"Any travel plans you have outside our area. You'll need to be at the inquest and give testimony."

"Inquest?" I said faintly.

"Yes, the enquiry where cause of death is determined. I'll

make sure you're informed of the date." He said goodbye and ended the call.

I carefully placed the phone on the table, a shaky, jittery feeling creeping over me. Quimby threw the words *inquest* and *testimony* around casually. I put my head in my hands. All in a day's work for him, but it wasn't normal for me. I didn't want to think about giving testimony or about causes of death.

"Excuse me, miss?"

I raised my head and saw Henry standing beside the table. "I don't know if you're hungry, but me mum said you look like you could do with a good crumpet." He set down a plate of warm rolls that looked a bit like English muffins. Dollops of melting butter oozed across the bumpy surfaces.

"Looks marvelous." I realized I was hungry, and the warm bread and melting butter looked so good. Carbs and fat—what better comfort food was there? I bit into the bread as Henry topped off my coffee.

"Shame about Mr. Dunn," Henry said.

"I know. I still can't quite believe it."

"Odd, too, about the spare tire." The dining area was empty, and Henry seemed to be in no hurry to get back to the kitchen.

"What do you mean?" I asked before popping another bite of crumpet in my mouth.

"Me mate who works at the garage said Mr. Dunn had a flat. He must have stopped off by the bridge to change it himself, but if the car was a hire he probably had breakdown cover. He could have called for service."

"Not Kevin. Instead of waiting around for someone, he'd rather do it himself." I brushed the crumbs from my fingers and sat back in my chair. "Well, that answers one of my questions—why he was stopped there by the bridge." Henry reached for the plate to remove it, and I said, "Thank you, Henry, you've given me more information than the detective chief inspector."

"Oh, if you want to know what happened you should talk to

Jeremy. His dad owns the garage. They towed the car out of the water. He stayed on and watched it all, the recovery of the body and everything." A dismayed look came over his face, and he added hastily, "Sorry. Don't know why I said that. Forgot there for a second that he was your boss and all."

"It's okay, Henry. Don't worry about it. If I can't get any answers out of the inspector, I might want to talk to your friend." I left the restaurant area, and as I crossed to the stairs, Doug looked up from some paperwork.

"Oh, got a package here for you. Came late yesterday. Sorry to hear about Mr. Dunn."

"Thank you." I took the cardboard box from him, wondering what Marci had sent me and how she'd gotten it here so fast.

"He was a fine man, always a nice word for all the staff." He shook his head and fussed with the papers. "I knew something wasn't right when he didn't come back that day. I should have called the constable."

"I wish I'd done the same thing." Would things have turned out differently if Marci and I hadn't concocted a plan to keep Kevin's disappearance secret? If we'd called the police right away would it have made a difference? When had Kevin stopped by the bridge to change the tire? If it was Friday, then by the time we figured out he was missing on Monday...well, the time to help him would have been long past, but what if it was more recent than that? Kevin had a car. He could have driven to a completely different part of England on Friday and only recently returned. I thought of the suitcase left behind and the go-bag. He wouldn't normally have gone off and left them, but if something came up—an emergency—he might have gone without them.

Kevin did go off-script occasionally. He could survive a day or two without his suitcase. He could pick up a toothbrush and change of clothes. I could picture him, grabbing what was most important, his camera and heading out on the spur-of-the-moment. What if he'd done that—gone somewhere outside of the immediate area around Nether Woodsmoor for a few days? If he had been on his way back via the road over the Parkview Hall bridge when he got a flat tire...

What if Kevin had been struggling to get out of the water, fighting the current and the tangling roots while I was here in England, poking about looking for him in pubs? My stomach turned with the thought as I climbed the stairs.

In my room, I dropped down onto the bed and fought down the nauseous feeling. If I had said something...if I had done things differently, would Kevin still be alive? I pulled Quimby's card from my pocket and stared at it. I wanted to call him and demand details, but if he wouldn't—or couldn't—tell me when Kevin's body would be released, then I doubted he'd tell me anything else. Maybe he wasn't sure what happened yet. Maybe that was why he was so cagey. I'd probably get more answers from Henry's buddy down at the local garage than from Quimby.

I put the card down and looked at the box in my lap. About ten inches square, it didn't have a return address or postmark on it. My name was printed in block letters above the name and address of the Old Nether Woodsmoor Inn. One long strip of clear packing tape held the box closed. I plucked at the edge of it until I had enough to grip it, then pulled it back and opened the flaps. My heartbeat did a little rumba. Inside, resting in a nest of crumpled newspaper, sat Kevin's camera.

CHAPTER 8

I RECOGNIZED IT IMMEDIATELY FROM the customized camera strap. Kevin had a personalized strap made with his name embroidered on it in red. The strap had been neatly accordion-folded and tucked into the space by the lens. The last few inches of the strap had been wrapped around the camera and held the folds in place. Even with only intermittent sections of the embroidery showing, I knew it was Kevin's camera. When I'd moved up from his assistant to a full-fledged scout, he'd presented me with my own personalized strap, but the embroidery on my strap was royal blue. Zara had one, too. Hers was purple.

I knew the right thing to do was leave the camera exactly where it was and call Quimby.

I sat there for a few seconds, chewing the inside of my lip. The 'new stuff' that Mr. O'Leery was waiting for could be sitting in my lap. If I called Quimby, he'd whisk the camera away, and it would go into evidence. I couldn't see Quimby immediately handing over copies of the photos to me. It might be years before we got the images back.

Of course, with Kevin gone, I didn't know if Premier Locations could hang onto the *P & P* job. I didn't even know if Premier Locations would exist in a few days or weeks, but if we were able to somehow go on, we'd need the photographs... if they were on the memory card.

And if there was anything on the memory card, it might show me what had happened to Kevin. It was a long shot, but...

I'd already touched the outside of the box, so I moved it to the bed, then I went to find my tweezers. I returned from the bathroom and used the tweezers to grip the strap. As I lifted it up, the weight of the camera caused the strap to unfold. I lowered the camera onto the bed with the memory card compartment facing me.

I blew out a calming breath, then gently used the chintz duvet to hold the camera steady with one hand while I pushed the tweezers against the button that held the compartment containing the memory card. The button slid up, I transferred the pressure to the right, and the compartment door popped open. Using the tweezers, I swung the door open, then gripped the memory card, which slid out smoothly. I had to work a bit to juggle the memory card into the card reader attached to my computer, but I managed to get it plugged into the slot without dropping it or touching it with my fingers.

The room phone rang, and I jumped guiltily. My first completely irrational thought was that it was Quimby calling, but I told myself not to be paranoid and answered it.

A deep voice came over the line. "Ms. Sharp? This is Henry. You left your phone on the table. If you'll be in your room for a few minutes, I'll run it up to you."

"Yes, I'll be here. Thanks."

I breathed deeply to slow my racing heart, then selected the drive on my computer and sat back as images downloaded, flashing across the screen, each one showing for only a second or two, creating a blur of quaint English country images, stately homes, and occasionally a shot of a person. The images were moving too quickly for me to distinguish much about them, but at this point, I was relieved there *were* images to download—that I hadn't tampered with evidence for no reason.

A knock sounded, and I opened the door, expecting Henry. Alex stood there, my phone in one hand, the other gripping a to-go cup of coffee. He had another lidded coffee cup tucked into the crook of one arm. I had a second of *déjà vu*. Today he wore a steel-colored sweater instead of a denim shirt, but he had on the same combat boots, jeans, and leather jacket, and his backpack was again draped on one shoulder. Had it only been a day since he'd stood in that same place?

He held out the phone. "Yours, I believe?"

"Yes, thanks." I fought my instinct to narrow the opening of the door and block Alex's view of the room. The computer was on the twin bed closest to the door, the screen positioned so that Alex would be able to see if he glanced inside the room.

He juggled the coffees then handed me one. "Henry was on his way up with your phone, but I told him I'd bring it since I was coming here anyway—" he broke off, a frown crinkling his forehead as he glanced over my shoulder. "Hey, isn't that Kevin's camera? And, oh, you're looking at the photos."

So much for keeping everything to myself. I opened the door wider and drew him in. "Yes. The camera came in that box. Arrived for me yesterday. No, don't touch it—it's evidence."

Alex raised his eyebrows. "Evidence?"

"In the investigation."

His eyebrows went up another notch.

I waved him to the chair by the window. "You haven't heard? I figured in a village this small, the news would be out in moments."

"Normally, it is, but I was busy this morning. Haven't talked to anyone. What happened?"

"A detective chief inspector showed up," I said, thinking of the Agatha Christie books I'd read. "At least, I'm pretty sure that was his title."

Alex said, "Sounds right. DCI, for short."

I continued. "Yes, that was it. DCI Quimby was waiting for me downstairs this morning. He wouldn't tell me much, only that Kevin's death wasn't an accident, but he had a ton of questions."

"That's…well, that's going to shake things up around here. They must suspect very strongly it was…" his voice trailed off.

My stomach clenched, but I steadied myself, taking a deep breath and blowing it out again before finishing his sentence. "Murder, yes. He didn't use that term, but what else could it be if it wasn't an accident?"

"Are you okay?" Alex was staring at me with that intense concentration that unnerved me. "Have you had something to eat today?"

"Yes, I ate."

Alex sipped his coffee, but kept his gaze on me. I perched on the edge of the bed. "Don't worry, I'm okay. It was…unsettling…once I heard from Quimby. When I realized that he suspected Kevin had been…murdered, I couldn't help wondering how recently had it happened? What if he went in the water while I was doing a pub-crawl, looking for him? Would it have made a difference if Marci and I had called the police the instant we realized something was wrong?" I rubbed my hand across my forehead. "I'm sorry, I don't know why I'm telling you all this. I usually have a better filter."

Alex put his coffee down and leaned forward, resting his arms on his knees. "There's one thing I know—you can destroy yourself playing the what-if game."

His tone had such intensity that I wondered what had happened to him. What "what-if" had he struggled with? He cleared his throat and transferred his gaze to the camera, then he glanced at Kevin's suitcase and go-bag stacked neatly along the wall. "So...his camera? It wasn't in his gear?"

"No. Doug said this box arrived late yesterday. I opened it, and when I saw it was Kevin's camera—well, I debated for about five seconds about handing it over to Quimby, but I decided I had to see if there were any photos on it. There were." I clicked a button on my laptop, and a grid of tiny thumbnails appeared.

Alex moved over and kneeled on the carpet in front of the computer as I went to the top of the list.

"Let's go slow," I said, "and look at each one carefully."

"Right. This one is Parkview Hall," he said. "Yes, these are the ones he took the second day. Everyone agreed it was perfect for Pemberley." The first photos were of the exterior of the house, capturing the grand home from various angles. Alex paused over a photo of Beatrice as she strode across the grounds, her dogs at her feet, golden Parkview Hall in the background.

A wave of sadness swept over me as I looked at the picture. "Kevin always liked to get a few shots of the people associated with the location. He told me it was because he was terrible with names, but that was just a cover. He was as interested in the people as he was the places. He especially liked it when he could get the two in the same shot, like this one with Parkview Hall."

"It's a nice one of Lady Stone."

"Lady Stone?" I asked.

"Yes. Sir Harold is a baronet. One of the oldest families in the area."

"She didn't say anything."

"No, she wouldn't. Not one to stand on ceremony is our Beatrice. Doesn't really want anyone to call her Lady Beatrice, in fact."

"That means a baronet served me tea. Oh my gosh. Should I have curtsied or something?"

"Nah, you and I, we're exempt. Americans. Fought a revolution, so we didn't have to, you know." I must have still looked stricken because Alex patted my arm, which sent a little shiver through me. "Don't worry. Beatrice hates pomp and circumstance." Did shock have aftereffects? Surely that was the reason for the sensation that sparked through me? Whatever was going on with me, it didn't seem to affect Alex at all.

He refocused on the laptop, and paged down a few lines. "Here's a good shot of Grove Cottage."

Before I could examine the next group of photos, the room phone rang. It was Doug informing me that Quimby was back, and wanted to speak with Alex. "I know he went up to your room a little while ago. Is he still with you?"

"Yes, I'll send him down."

I hung up and turned to Alex. "Your turn with the DCI."

We didn't look at the rest of the photos. Since Quimby was back, I needed to hand off the camera to him, as well as Kevin's other things, and that meant I had to get the memory card back inside the camera.

Alex went down to speak to Quimby, and I set about saving the photos to my hard drive as well as cloud storage. Then I carefully returned the memory card to the camera. Getting the compartment door closed with the tweezers was considerably more difficult than getting it open had been, but I managed to do it without directly touching the camera. I replaced it in the box, then quickly went through Kevin's suitcase and go-bag to make sure there wasn't anything that could possibly be related to his death, but again, it was a normal suitcase and the go-bag didn't have anything special tucked away in a secret compartment.

I squared my shoulders and dialed the front desk, asking if Doug could help me carry some bags downstairs. I could have carried them myself—Lord knows, I'd schlepped my bags around enough that I could have gotten Kevin's bag downstairs on my own, but I wanted to ask Doug a few things.

As he slung the go-bag over one shoulder and gripped the suitcase handle, I carefully picked up the box, trying not to deposit any more fingerprints on it than I had already unintentionally left. "In the lobby, you said?" Doug asked.

"Yes, I'm sure the police will want to look at them." I followed him into the hall, shutting the door to my room firmly behind me. "About this box, you said it arrived last night?"

Doug moved delicately down the stairs, holding the suitcase so that it didn't bump the wall. "Yes. I went up to show a couple to their room, and when I came back down it was on the counter."

"Was anyone else on duty at the front desk then?"

"No, Henry and Tara were busy with the dinner crowd."

We arrived in the lobby area, and I examined the ceiling, but it was bare except for heavy wooden beams spaced along the whitewashed ceiling. "I don't suppose you have any cameras or monitoring in here, do you?"

He placed the bags in front of the counter and looked up, surprised. "No. No need. We're a family operation, except for the maids who come in daily to do the rooms, but they don't work behind the counter."

"I see." I propped the box on top of the suitcase.

"No need to worry. You're safe as houses here in Nether Woodsmoor. No one has any trouble here."

"Except for Kevin," I murmured more to myself than to Doug, but he heard me.

"Yes, terrible business, that. But he wasn't from around here. His trouble must have followed him. It couldn't be anything to do with us here."

Steps sounded on the hardwood, and Quimby and Alex turned the corner from the restaurant, stepping into the lobby area. Quimby was handing over his business card and telling Alex to call him if anything else came to mind. The two men halted at the counter.

I pointed to the bags. "I had these brought down. They were Kevin's. I figured you'd want to have a look. Doug handed them off to me when I arrived. He'd held them here after Kevin checked out. It didn't occur to me until after you'd left this morning that you'd want them."

"Indeed," Quimby murmured, his gaze shifting from the bags to Doug, who had stepped behind the counter.

"I kept them here," Doug said. "Didn't know what to do with them, but then I got the message Ms. Sharp was arriving and would take charge of them. I had no idea he'd done a runner."

Quimby looked back at me. "You've gone through them?"

"Yes, as soon as I arrived. I'd hoped there would be something to indicate where he was, but I didn't find anything. His laptop is password protected. His camera wasn't with his things. It arrived yesterday in that box. I opened it this morning after Doug gave it to me."

Doug explained how the box had appeared on the counter the evening before when the desk was unattended. Quimby took out a pen, opened a flap, and peered inside the box. "You've touched it, I suppose?"

"Only the outside of the box before I realized what was in it." I stopped there, leaving out the tweezer-assisted memory card extraction. I wondered if the police had a way to see if data had been downloaded from a memory card? I hoped not. If they somehow discovered I'd downloaded the photos, I'd have to admit to giving in to my curiosity, but I wasn't about to mention it now. He must have used the pen to press the camera's power button because I heard the familiar whirr and click. "Doesn't appear to have been in the water." He turned off the power and replaced his pen in his pocket. "When you first went through Mr. Dunn's belongings did you think it strange that the camera wasn't there?"

"Not really. Kevin usually took it with him in case he ran across something he wanted to photograph. I assumed he had it with him."

Quimby said he'd have his sergeant pick up the bags. "If I might have another word with you two." His gaze pinged between Alex and me. "Perhaps outside?"

The three of us moved to the little courtyard area, which was empty. Quimby said, "I want you both to understand the seriousness of this situation. A man is dead. It is of utmost importance that you share fully any association you have."

Alex and I shared a confused glance. "What are you hinting at?" I asked.

Quimby looked at the second story of the inn to my room's window. "You say, Ms. Sharp, that you arrived here on Tuesday and met Mr. Norcutt the following morning, but you had no acquaintance with him before that, yet you spent the whole day yesterday in his company. Doug Owens informs me that you both spent considerable time in Ms. Sharp's room together. In fact, that is where you were this morning, Mr. Norcutt, instead of at your home office. Perhaps I should have phrased it differently and asked what your *relationship* is?"

I blinked, stunned at what he was insinuating. Here I had been worrying about leaving out the detail about downloading the photos, but Quimby had jumped to the conclusion that Alex and I were involved.

"Kate is a business associate," Alex said, his words clipped. "It is common to spend time—days at a time—together in our line of work. Talk to Doug. He will tell you I did the same thing when Mr. Dunn, Mr. O'Leery, and the rest of the scouting group were here. We spent almost every moment together. As far as this morning, I came by to check on Kate. I will admit that I was concerned about her. Yesterday was a very traumatic day. Dealing with death generally is difficult, at least for those of us who don't encounter it every day."

Quimby replied in his same bland tone, "I see." He looked at me, waiting for my reply.

"Of course, what Alex says is true. I met Alex the day after I arrived. I told him that Kevin had disappeared, and Alex agreed to help me look for him."

"So you had no contact with Mr. Norcutt before arriving in England?" I opened my mouth to reply, but he held up a hand, warningly. "Think carefully. We can search email, phone records, and web chats."

"I don't need to think carefully. I didn't know him or communicate with him in any way—phone, text, email, whatever. In fact, I keep forgetting his last name. What are you insinuating? That somehow Alex and I knew each other before this week?"

"You told me that one of the employees of Premier Locations might either take over the business or simply take the contacts and open their own business," Quimby said. "Perhaps you enlisted a partner, say in another country, to help you, even convinced him to commit a crime when you were not in the country, giving you an alibi. In return, you promised to allow him to join you in your new business venture." Quimby looked toward Alex as he said, "Inquiries about your business indicate it is on rather precipitous ground, financially."

"Which is all the more reason for Alex and me to want Kevin alive," I said. "Things are always unstable in the movie business, but Kevin knew Mr. O'Leery. They had a friendship that went back a long way; it was one of the reasons Mr. O'Leery picked Kevin as the location scout. There is no guarantee at all that Mr. O'Leery would use Alex or me—either together or separately—as a replacement for Kevin. But this whole line of thought is...crazy." My heartbeat had been pounding steadily as my anger rose as I spoke. I couldn't keep the tremor out of my voice. "First, you accuse me of having an affair with Kevin, which is absurd, and now you accuse me and Alex of the same thing and tack on a plot to kill Kevin, which is —well, it's beyond absurd."

Quimby's green eyes bored into me, and I felt as if he was mentally taking note of my agitated state: *subject became quite incensed at the suggestion she had a hand in the victim's death.*

"Motives for murder often seem inexplicable on the surface," he said mildly. "In any investigation we always look to the people closest to the victim. And even you have to admit that the timing of Mr. Dunn's disappearance and your arrival are interesting, as well as the fact that you have formed such a close working relationship with Mr. Norcutt in an extremely short acquaintance."

"But—"

Quimby spoke over me. "Then we have the sudden appearance of Mr. Dunn's camera, which you admit was in your possession. It conveniently appeared at a time when no one was able to observe the delivery. A time, which you admitted during our earlier interview, that you were in the inn. You told me Mr. Dunn's habit of keeping his camera about his person, yet it was not in the car, or on his person, or in the river. It was here in your possession." He tipped his head forward as he said, "Sorry to have offended you, but I must explore all avenues." He returned to the inn.

I was fuming at his accusations, but a cold tendril of fear curled through me.

CHAPTER 9

I SPUN AWAY FROM THE inn, strode off through the parking lot, then took the path that ran along the main road, but turned away from the village. I saw the signpost for the walking trail that Doug had mentioned. I jogged across the road and made for the path. Heavy footsteps thudded behind me, and then Alex came abreast of me on the hard packed dirt lane. "That was pretty intense back there. You okay?"

I picked up my pace, moving along an aged stone wall that lined the trail. "You shouldn't have followed me," I said over my shoulder as Alex dropped back. "Quimby probably noticed it and added it to the list of things we've done that are suspicious."

Alex caught back up. "Who cares? Everything he's got is circumstantial."

I whirled to face him. "I care. Don't you see that every moment Quimby spends focused on you and me takes him away from finding out who really killed Kevin?" I resumed my brisk pace.

The path angled away from the road through an open field,

the ground rising gently, but steadily. By the time I reached the apex of the small hill where the path led to a stile over another stone wall, I was out of breath. Instead of going over the stile, I clambered onto the stone wall and sat down, my feet dangling a few inches above the ground. The day was overcast and darker than yesterday with low gray clouds. The coolness of the stone seeped into the back of my legs. Alex climbed up beside me.

I sat a moment, taking in the view. The ground dipped rather steeply to the yellow stone house Alex had shown me yesterday. Grove Cottage nestled in the hollow at the base of the hill. We were looking at the side of the house, and I could see the exterior brickwork for the chimney as well as a stretch of gardens in the back. A thick line of trees ringed the back of the property.

We weren't that far from the main road, and I could still hear the faint swoosh of traffic, but the noise didn't spoil the beautiful scene. Just looking at the view calmed and steadied me. I shifted so that I could look back over the wall to the path we'd walked. The tiny squares of the village clustered by the silvery curve of the river. Stone walls crisscrossed the rolling green hills at all angles, creating patches in slightly different shades of green, making the whole countryside look as if someone had tossed a quilt over it. Fuzzy white dots—sheep—speckled some of the distant hills.

I blew out a breath. "Sorry about that, back there." The wind whipped up, and I reached up to pull my hair out of my face as I looked at Alex. "I didn't mean to snap at you."

He waved away my apology. "It's fine. I have a thick hide. What you should apologize for is that bruising pace you set. An impromptu hike up Strange Hill is quite a workout, especially after a full breakfast."

I had to smile at his exaggeration. He'd been breathing hard like me when we reached the wall, but he'd recovered just as quickly as I had. I looked out over the quiet countryside. "I just had to get away. I do that when I'm stressed. There's something about being out, looking at the trees, the grass, the sky." I shook my head. "I don't know how to describe it. It just helps." I shifted a bit on the wall. "Why is it called Strange Hill?"

Tendrils of ivy clung to the stone wall. Alex picked up a dried ivy leaf and rolled the stem in his fingers. He pointed to Grove Cottage below us. "That used to be called Strange House. All of this area was owned by the Strange family. Old-timers in the village still call it that."

"What happened?"

"Becca renamed it. Apparently 'Strange House' didn't set the right tone for her country estate."

I smiled. "I can see why she'd want to change it. Grove Cottage is much more English country home-ish." I heard a noise and turned to see two people approaching, a man and a woman, both dressed in outdoor gear—rain coats, hiking boots, and backpacks. They nodded a greeting, climbed over the stile, and continued down the path that turned away from us and ran along the stone wall. They followed it, dropping down the hill's descent until we couldn't see them anymore.

"Ramblers," Alex explained. "Hikers."

"Aren't they on private property?" I asked, assuming that Grove Cottage's land stretched to the stone wall.

"Yes and no. The stone wall is the property line, but the footpath is a public right of way. Anyone can walk on it. Public footpaths have a long tradition here. Property owners can't obstruct or shut down the footpaths."

"So you can stroll around the countryside—that's wonderful."

Alex turned toward me. "I understand that a police investigation is upsetting, and the questions were—well—awkward, but Quimby is only doing his job."

I kept my gaze on the patchwork of rolling green hills. "I

was in grad school when my dad divorced my mom. That doesn't sound like a big deal—happens all the time, right? But it devastated my mom. She's...fragile. Actually, she's as tough as an old boot, but she *thinks* she's fragile. I had to move from San Diego to L.A. and give up grad school. It was supposed to be temporary. The plan was to move back to L.A. for a few months to help my mom get back on her feet and work to save some money so I could go back to school. But then my dad fell off the edge of the earth. Disappeared. The alimony stopped and my mother was not prepared to earn a living, to put it mildly. I wasn't either. Turns out, an undergraduate degree in English Literature and Language isn't a thing human resources people jump at. Anyway, after a year of living on mac and cheese and Ramen noodles and lying awake at night wondering how long it would be before the landlord evicted us, I ran into Kevin. He needed an assistant. I'd been working temp jobs and falling farther and farther behind on my student loans and the rent on my mom's tiny condo. Kevin took me on, taught me a marketable skill that allowed me to survive. He was there for me when things were bad, and I'm not about to sit around and wait for the police to figure out I'm not the one who hurt him—"

The roar of a heavy engine cut through the quiet. It grew louder as it neared, and I twisted to look along the wall in the opposite direction from the way hikers had gone. A white SUV came into view, pausing at a gate. A mechanism whirred to life, the gates swung open, and the SUV accelerated through them only to come to a sharp stop.

The driver door opened, and a thirtyish woman with voluptuous curves and a cloud of reddish-gold hair hopped out.

"Becca Ford," Alex murmured to me as he stood and tossed the dry leaf away.

I scooted off the wall as well. "Ah, the friend of the production with lots of ideas."

"Alex," Becca called as she made her way to us, leaving the car door open, an annoying warning ding pulsing through the air. She wore a hip-length caramel-colored trench coat. The belt was cinched tight at her waist, which showed off her figure. Riding breeches hugged her legs, and leather boots came up to her calves. She barreled along the trail, flicking mud on her boots and the lower edge of her coat. A gauzy scarf trailed off one shoulder. It caught on a bush, and she impatiently jerked it off the prickly branches. I figured that scarf—a designer brand—probably cost more than a car payment, but she didn't give it a second look. "I thought that was you," she said to Alex.

She ran a quick glance over me, but she must have decided I wasn't worthy of her attention because she fixed her gaze on Alex as she stopped in front of him. "Do you need more photos?" She pressed his arm. "You know you're welcome anytime at Grove Cottage."

Alex shifted, causing her hand to fall away. "That's very kind of you, Mrs. Ford," he said formally, and I tilted my head to study him. I hadn't heard him speak in that tone of voice.

She pouted, sticking out her collagen-enhanced lips, which were covered with a heavy layer of apricot lipstick. Living in Southern California and working with movie and television people, I'd picked up a smidgen of knowledge about plastic surgery and other enhancements. Becca's lips, like so many of the fixes, had all the subtly of a poorly done CGI sequence.

"How many times do I have to tell you? Call me Becca."

"At least once more."

She flicked a glance at me and shook her head, "He's oh-so-proper." She looked back to Alex. "You don't call Beatrice, Lady Stone."

"Because she would flay me alive, if I did."

The pout reappeared. Alex added, "And I can't call the most

beautiful young woman in Nether Woodsmoor by her first name. Think of the rumors."

I looked down at my feet to hide a smile. Obviously, Becca Ford's weak point was vanity, and Alex knew how to work the flattery to keep her happy.

She tapped his shoulder playfully. "You exaggerate, but I love it. So, any news on my idea?"

For one second, Alex had that deer in the headlights look, but he recovered almost instantly. "Gilding the ceiling of the entrance? I'm afraid it's a no-go."

Her shoulders sagged. "Is everything a 'no' with these people? Don't they realize I don't like it when I don't get my way? Well, you must have some news for me, since you're here."

Alex and I exchanged a glance. He raised his eyebrows a fraction of an inch, and I knew he was asking me if he should tell her about Kevin. I gave him a little nod. There was no need to try to keep anything a secret. In fact, I was surprised she didn't already know about Kevin's death.

Becca picked up on the nonverbal exchange, and I could tell she didn't like it. She ran a slower, more assessing look over me, her blue eyes narrowing as if she were examining something on a sales rack that didn't meet her standards.

"This is my colleague, Kate Sharp," Alex said.

Her face relaxed into a bright smile. "Oh, you're one of the film people. How delightful."

"There is some news," Alex said. "You haven't heard about Mr. Dunn?"

Her coquettish manner faded slightly, and she said quickly, "No, I ran up to London. I stayed in the flat there. I had a look at the plans for the visitor's kiosk."

"Visitor's kiosk?" Alex asked.

"We'll have to have somewhere to collect the fees from the scads of tourists who will be arriving, you know." She frowned suddenly. "I am worried about coach parking, though. It will be a bit of a squeeze on the road." She flicked a hand. "But never mind that now. I'll work that out with the council. What did I miss? I'm just arriving back now."

"It's sad news, I'm afraid. Mr. Dunn has died."

Her blue eyes widened. She had been constantly moving, fiddling with her hair, and fingering a dangling thread where a button was missing on her coat, but now she went still. "Oh, that's terrible. When…did it happen?"

"We don't know exactly. Sometime after Friday. The police are investigating," I said.

"Why? What happened?"

"That's just it—no one knows what happened," Alex said. "His car was in the river near the bridge by Parkview Hall, but he was found downstream."

She looked away from us, out over the hills and murmured, "Then that means…" She refocused on Alex. "What does it mean for the production?"

I was almost sure that she'd been about to say something else, but changed her mind. "We don't know yet. Things are still being sorted out," I said. "Were you going to say something? Something about Kevin?"

"Yes. Yes, I was." She smoothed down her coat and tightened the belt. "I wasn't going to say anything, but I've changed my mind. You should know I won't give up. I don't care what Kevin said. It's terrible that he's dead. Quite shocking and tragic and all that, but we had a verbal contract. Grove Cottage *will be* Longbourn." Her playful flirting had vanished. She was coldly serious, her puffy lips mashed into a grim line. I made a mental note to tell Marci that if the production went on, Alex needed a raise.

"I'm sorry, I don't understand." Alex glanced from Becca to me. "What do you mean?"

She rolled her eyes. "Mr. Dunn's second thoughts. I was

really quite put out with you, Alex, that you didn't talk him out of it before he came here again."

"He came here? Without me?"

"Yes. You should have stopped him before he even considered the idea of changing."

Alex held up a hand. "Wait. Changing what?"

"The location, of course. Said he was having second thoughts and wanted another look," she said, her tone incredulous as if Kevin had decided to change the location to some absurd place like the moon.

I stepped closer. "So Kevin came back here on his own. When was this?"

"Friday afternoon."

"What happened?" I asked.

"He walked around the house and left."

"Did he say anything? Mention where he was going when he left?"

"No, he wouldn't even come inside."

CHAPTER 10

I PROBABLY OFFENDED BECCA FORD with my abrupt departure, but I didn't care.

"Hey, wait up," Alex called from behind me. I turned back, spotted him sprinting down the slope of Strange Hill, Becca a small figure at the top, watching us.

While I waited for him, I pulled my cell phone out of my pocket and sent a text to Marci. Alex caught up, and I resumed my quick pace.

"I see you want the full hill-walking workout—up and down at a jogging pace."

I threw a smile at him as I said, "No, I only want to get back to the inn."

He looked at my cell phone. "What's going on? Everything okay?"

"Yes. I sent a text to Marci, asking what she knows about Kevin and Frank Revel's history. I should have done that yesterday. I also want to find out what else Kevin did Friday afternoon. If he visited Grove Cottage did he go anywhere else?"

I could feel Alex's gaze on me as we resumed walking. "What?"

"You're a real take-charge kind of person, aren't you?" he said. "You know Quimby is going to check into Revel and Mr. Dunn's past and that he'll try to reconstruct Mr. Dunn's movements."

"That's what he should do, but if those questions he asked are any indication of how he investigates, then he's going to be so scattered all over the place that something really important could slip by him. I know I had nothing to do with Kevin's death, and I don't think you did—stop me now if I'm wrong, but my gut says you're in the clear."

"No, I swear I had nothing to do with it."

"Good. Just checking, you know."

"No offense taken. You only met me yesterday, so I can see how you might not trust me implicitly...yet."

"So, there you go. We're both innocent, but Quimby is obviously taking the time to investigate us, poking around to check out our stories, which is eating up time. All the while, the real trail that Quimby should be looking for is getting colder and colder. You know what they say about police investigations, that the first two days are critical. By the time Quimby eliminates us and focuses his attention where it should be, it may be too late."

"Some important clue will have disappeared?" Alex said.

"Possibly. Or been hidden or destroyed."

"I think you're not giving Quimby enough credit. You don't think he can pursue multiple leads?"

"He may be doing that, but if there's anything I can do to move the investigation along, I'm going to do it. I mean, what else am I going to do? I'm certainly not going to tour the English countryside—as beautiful as it is—and I'm not going to sit around twiddling my thumbs in my room, waiting for Quimby to call with news."

"You don't seem to be the thumb-twiddling sort."

"You're laughing at me," I said.

"No, I can understand the need to do something. I think you should be careful. I doubt Quimby will look kindly on anyone 'helping' him."

My phone rang. "It's Marci," I said, halting so I could answer it.

"How are you holding up, kid?"

"I'm okay," I said, realizing it was true. After the emotional dust-up that Quimby's accusations had caused, just deciding to take action, to do something proactive had steadied me. "What about you?"

"Things are falling apart here. The news is out. That's why I'm up early. Trying to do some damage control."

"What does Mr. O'Leery say?"

"Haven't heard from him since I broke the news. He said he'd get back to me." Her gusty sigh came over the line. "And I'm hearing rumblings about funding trouble. You know what that means."

"It may not be that bad. Mr. O'Leery may really be trying to sort out everything."

Marci snorted. "Sure, honey, you keep thinking that way. In the meantime, dust off the résumé. I know I'm updating mine today. I told Zara and Lori to do the same."

I asked, "So is anyone making noises about possibly starting up their own company? Or trying to take over Premier Locations?"

"No. Why do you ask? Are *you* thinking of it?"

"No, just something that has come up in the investigation. They're looking for motive."

"Well, if someone…did away with…Kevin to get control of Premier Locations, it was the stupidest move someone could have made. I probably shouldn't say anything, but it's all going to come out anyway. I think you already suspected how tight we were running."

"Yeah, I wondered." *So much for one of Quimby's theories.*

"Now if they're looking for motive. I've got a doozy for them. Frank Revel and Kevin were partners. They opened Premier Locations together fifteen years ago. They had a falling out over a woman—couldn't find out her name—then they went their separate ways. Kevin got the business, and Revel left town."

"How do you know all this? You weren't there, were you?"

"No. That was way before my time, but I've heard the rumors. Kevin still has his original business records in those dented filing cabinets behind his door. I did a little digging to make sure I wasn't passing along gossip, and it was all in there. The original incorporation papers as well as the ones where Frank Revel had his name removed from the company."

"Wow. Okay, I think you should send those to the DCI investigating the case."

"I've contacted the police here and found out the UK police have already been in touch with L.A.'s finest. A police officer is on the way to pick up the files. I guess they'll send the files on once they have a look at them."

After agreeing to check in with each other later in the day, we hung up, and I recapped the conversation for Alex as we resumed walking.

"So maybe Quimby *is* working all the aspects of the case," Alex said.

"Yes, that is a good sign, but he hasn't talked to Becca."

Alex said, "I'm surprised Kevin went back without me. I had the impression that he and Mr. O'Leery were extremely happy with the locations. They'd finalized the list only a day before. How could he have had second thoughts?"

"Kevin always had second thoughts. And third and fourth thoughts, too. He constantly scanned the horizon, looking for better options. Did you mention…what was her name—Eva?—to him?"

"Eve. Eve Wallings." Alex's pace slowed fractionally. "Yes, I think I did say something about Coventry House—only a passing reference."

"That would be enough for Kevin." I sighed. "He always loved a challenge. I can totally see him going out on his own, giving everything one last look and then making an attempt to get another, better location."

We reached the inn, and I hustled inside. The front desk was empty, but Doug was coming down the stairs, carrying a stack of linens. I asked if Quimby was still around.

"No, he left after talking to you."

"Thank you," I said and turned to Alex. "Looks like I'll have to call him."

Alex reached for his phone. "I'll do it. After all, I know Becca Ford. I don't know if she'll actually follow through and talk to the police on her own." Alex lowered his voice as he patted his pockets. "Becca tends to have selective memory issues. I know I put Quimby's card away somewhere."

"Becca? I thought she was Mrs. Ford to you," I said, unable to keep the teasing tone out of my voice.

"Formality is my first line of defense. And with her, I need as many lines of defense as possible."

"Oh, I think she will go to the police."

"Why?"

"The investigating officer is a male."

"Hmm, I should have emphasized that," Alex murmured. "Where is that business card?"

"I left the one Quimby gave me in my room. Come on, I'll get it for you."

"Is that a good idea?" Alex asked.

"What?" I stopped, my foot poised on the first step. "Oh. Quimby's insinuations." I ran my hand over the carved pineapple that topped the newel post, weighing if I wanted to answer more questions from Quimby, but then a burst of anger hit me. Alex and I hadn't done anything wrong. I couldn't second-guess my every move, wondering how it looked. "Oh, forget all that. I need you upstairs."

Alex followed me up the stairs. "There are so many replies to that statement. Too bad I'm a gentleman."

"All of them in bad taste, I'm sure. Better that you keep them to yourself. What I should have said was that I need to show you something upstairs in my room."

"Better and better," Alex murmured.

I rolled my eyes as I opened the door to my room. I slid Quimby's card off the table and handed it to Alex. He dialed, then came to look over my shoulder as I picked up my laptop. The screensaver was up, rotating quotes. Alex, the phone tilted away from his mouth, read one aloud as he waited for Quimby to answer. "I am excessively diverted."

"It's a quote from—"

"*Pride and Prejudice*. Yes, I recognize it. I like the line about poetry driving away love." He pulled the phone closer. "DCI Quimby, Alex Norcutt here." He recapped our conversation with Becca Ford, paused, and finally said, "Very good, I'll wait for his call."

"Quimby will have Detective Sergeant Olney call me back to get Becca's contact info." Alex pocketed his phone. "Kevin's photos? That's what you wanted to show me?"

"Yes. I want you to look at the rest of them. Kevin usually had his camera with him, and he was continually snapping photos—not always potential locations. Sometimes he'd take pictures of people, like the candid photos of Beatrice. Other times, he'd take photos of the signs along the way to a location, or the restaurant where we had lunch, or the clouds."

"So you think he unintentionally documented his movements on Friday?"

"Yes, that's why I need you here. So you can tell me where the photos were taken."

"Don't you think this is something for Quimby?"

I had been paging through the photos, but I stopped. "If there's something here, then yes," I said reluctantly. I didn't want to have to explain how I had a copy of the photos from Kevin's camera. "First things first. Is there anything here that Quimby would be interested in?"

I returned to the thumbnails and skimmed down to the photos of Beatrice then slowed as I came to the next photos.

"Those do look like new photos of Grove Cottage." Alex sunk into the bed beside me, his warm thigh pressing against mine. I shifted the laptop so he could see the screen and inched to the side without allowing myself to think about why. "The light is different from when I took him there," he said. "The light is stronger than when I showed Grove Cottage to him and Mr. O'Leery."

I enlarged the photos and we looked at each one, but they were only exterior shots of the house, and then some of the thick line of trees that enclosed the back of the property.

One photo captured a bit of crumbled stone wall. I looked at Alex, and he shrugged.

"No idea. There are thousands of places that could have been taken around here—lots of dry stone walls."

I moved to the next photo.

"But I do know where that one is," Alex said. "That's Coventry House. And that photo was taken *inside* the gates."

CHAPTER 11

"IT IS A GORGEOUS LOCATION," I said, studying the three-storied, gabled home with ivy climbing up the gray stone exterior to mullioned windows. A garden with graveled paths, evergreen shrubs, and low boxwoods ran along each side of the main entrance framing a circle drive. Farther away from the house, hardwood trees lined the edge of the property, their branches shading the stone wall and gates.

"How did he get inside those gates?" Alex murmured to himself as he paged through to the last photo. "No more photos after the ones of Coventry House, by the way."

"He probably asked," I said.

"Eve wouldn't have let him in. Not unless she didn't know he was a location scout..." Alex's voice trailed off questioningly.

I shook my head. "Kevin was always up front. He never tried to put something over on people. He always said that if you started out lying to people, it never ended well."

"That's true, but I don't see how he got in there. I suppose his high moral standards extended to sneaking in as well?"

"Of course he wouldn't do that. What good would that do? It would only make the owner angrier."

"Yes, you're right." He rubbed his hand across his mouth, still staring at the laptop. "I can't see how he could have skirted Eve."

"I think we should ask."

"Go to Coventry House?"

"Why not? Besides figuring out Kevin's movements on Friday, these photos could be the 'new stuff' that Mr. O'Leery is waiting for. I need to find out if Kevin talked with the Wallings."

"Eve Wallings didn't mention it yesterday when we saw her at breakfast," Alex said.

"No, but she didn't seem interested in talking at all...to you."

One corner of Alex's mouth turned up. "Very true. She's impervious to my charms."

"If Kevin talked to the Wallings, that affects the production. If the production is affected, I need to know about it. It's a long shot that Premier Locations will still be the location scout and manager, but if it works out, I need to be up to speed on what Kevin did."

"Excellent point." Alex handed me the laptop. "I'll drive."

"What about informing Quimby? A moment ago you were all for dropping these photos in his lap and walking away."

He had his hand on the doorknob, his car keys already in his hand. "Turn about is fair play, is that what you're thinking?" He stepped away from the door. "Okay, yes, I admit it. I have an interest in seeing how Kevin got around Eve, and that makes me less anxious to coordinate our moves with the police." He looked around, spotted Quimby's business card, and swiped it off the table in a smooth movement, extending it to me. "You get to call this time."

I plucked the card from his hand. "Okay, you called my

bluff. The last thing I want to do is tell Quimby where I got these photos, but I suppose I must." I squared my shoulders and dialed. After three rings, it went to voicemail. Relieved, I left Quimby a message, telling him we'd found photos that Kevin had taken Friday afternoon at Coventry House. "I'll be happy to give the details to your sergeant when he calls Alex back."

"You look so innocent, but you're actually quite devious," Alex said after I hung up.

"What do you mean?" I shrugged into my coat. One of my sleeves was inside out.

Alex moved to hold the coat as I worked my arm into the sleeve, then he settled it on my shoulders, his hands brushing over my arms. "You thought I wouldn't notice that you glossed over where you found the photos?"

"You're too observant by half." I flicked my hair over the collar and headed for the door.

"You're quiet," Alex said, his hands on the wheel as he negotiated the turns in the road.

"Sorry, just thinking."

Even though the sun was out, it was much cooler than yesterday, and Alex hadn't even asked about putting the top down on the convertible. There had been a fresh scatter of papers on the passenger seat and a few new sticky notes on the dash. Alex had swept them all up and dumped them in the growing pile in the trunk.

"The quiet doesn't bother me," he said. "Not when it's a comfortable quiet."

It was true that there was a relaxed, amiable atmosphere in the car. I twisted toward him. "I was thinking about Frank Revel and Kevin."

He nodded, and we covered a few more miles in silence

before I said, "It doesn't make sense. Even if there had been a rift between Frank and Kevin, why would Frank go after Kevin now...years later?"

"Some people hold grudges. You know that saying about revenge."

"A dish best served cold, yes. But it seems so extreme...to go after Kevin fifteen years later. Clearly, Kevin didn't end up with the woman—whoever she was—because he wasn't in a relationship with anyone now. And, if Frank Revel did go after Kevin, it's so sloppy. He was one of the last people seen with Kevin. Surely if he was going to exact some sort of revenge, it would make more sense to wait and not do it after a very public argument."

"Crime of passion?" Alex asked. "Revel was quite emotional when you asked him about Kevin. Perhaps it was unplanned."

"I suppose it could have happened that way." I shifted in my seat. "You know, we still don't know *what* really happened. How did Kevin end up in the water, but out of his submerged car? Maybe I should talk to Henry's friend at the garage."

"Jeremy?"

"Henry said Jeremy was there when they...found Kevin."

"Jeremy's a good kid. He might have noticed something."

"Is it far?"

"Nothing is very far in Nether Woodsmoor." Alex made a few turns that took us down the narrow streets of a residential area with modest two-story duplex homes. Mixed in with the aged stone houses were a few modern stucco homes. We cruised down the street, flying by gardens enclosed by stone walls until we came to a stone building set back from the road behind two gas pumps. Alex parked off to the side of the gas pumps, and we both climbed out of the car. I headed for the half of the building with a glass door that led to a waiting area, but Alex tilted his head to the double wooden doors, one of which had been folded back into the shop area. "They'll be in here."

I changed course and joined him at the doorway. In the dim garage area, two men were leaning over the open hood of a car while a third dug through a toolbox. He spotted us, picked up a rag, and moved in our direction while wiping his hands. He was young, probably barely out of his teens, and moved with the lanky grace of an athlete. He wore a dark vest over a blue coverall with a few streaks of grease on it. "Having trouble with the MG again, Mr. Norcutt?"

Alex looked at me. "Can you tell I am a familiar sight around here? Jeremy and his dad have resurrected the old MG more times than I can count. But for once, I'm not here about my car. This is Kate Sharp. She's staying at the inn. Henry thought she should talk to you. She worked with Mr. Dunn."

His easy smile faded at the mention of the name. He'd been rubbing the rag quickly across his hands, but now he stopped and crossed his arms. "That was a sad business to be sure. I've seen a few smash-ups, but nothing like that."

"Do you mind if I ask you a couple of questions about it?" I didn't want to press him, if it would upset him. "The police haven't told me anything. I just want to find out what happened, but only if you want to talk about it."

"Oh, I don't mind talking about it, but I don't think they were sure what happened either."

"What do you mean?"

Jeremy leaned against the stone wall of the building. "We pulled the car out, and we expected him to be in it, right?" He glanced at me, studying my face. I suppose to see if his words upset me, but I nodded at him to continue. "So when he wasn't there, they started the search. By the time they'd found him, we had the car secured. My dad sent me down to get the clearance to leave, but they'd found...the body and were focused on getting him out of the water. They didn't have time to talk to me, so I had to wait. I saw the whole thing."

"What did you see?" I asked, bracing myself.

"He was stuck under a thick tree root near the river bank, half in and half out of the water. It took them a while to get him out and when they did, I stayed back, out of their way. He didn't look very human—all swollen up and—"

Alex moved, and Jeremy broke off, but I said, "No, go ahead." I swallowed. "It's not easy to hear, but I want to know. Do you think that means he was in the water...a while?"

"Yes. I heard the emergency lads say so. They didn't know how long exactly, just that it wasn't recent. Sounded like more than a few hours. Anyway, the medical bloke, was there, too. He looked him over, and said there had been a blow to the back of the head and that he had a broken leg as well. Things calmed down after that, and I got clearance to leave."

I frowned, trying to make sense of it all. How did Kevin get a broken leg and a head injury? Was he in some sort of fight?

I realized Alex was talking and tuned back into the conversation. "...notice anything about the car? Did he have some sort of car trouble, do you think?"

"Yes, Henry mentioned something about a spare tire?" I asked.

"Hard to tell, with it being in the water and all, if he had car trouble. We didn't look it over or anything, but the back passenger tire had been changed. Maybe that was why he stopped."

He couldn't think of anything else to add, so I thanked him for talking to me. Once we were back in Alex's car, I stared out the window. In only a few minutes we left the residential neighborhood and were zipping through the rolling country-side with stone fences, hedges, and an occasional sheep flicking by, but I wasn't really looking at the scenery. "From what Jeremy said, it almost sounds as if Kevin was in a fight."

"Are you thinking of Frank Revel?" Alex asked.

I shrugged. "I don't know. Frank was angry with us when he spoke to us, but would he go after Kevin—hit him in the back of the head? Frank seemed more like an in-your-face guy. A confrontational type."

"That was the vibe I got, too."

"If Kevin was attacked, maybe he jumped into the water to get away. No, wait. That wouldn't make sense with a broken leg. Unless he broke his leg jumping in the water? But that doesn't sound like Kevin either. I have more questions now than ever. Let's go back to the pictures. At least those are concrete and can definitely tell us something."

Alex downshifted and turned onto a lane that led to closed iron gates. "Here's Coventry House."

The pillars on each side of the gate looked a little tottery— as if a stone might tumble out at any moment, but the gates themselves had a glossy coat of black paint and a modern intercom box perched on a pole a few feet back from the gate.

"Here goes nothing." Alex wound down his window and pressed the button.

We waited then he pressed the button again.

"No one home?" I ventured.

"Eve goes out, but Tom Wallings hardly ever leaves."

The line crackled, and we both jumped. "Alex Norcutt to see Eve Wallings, please," Alex said in an upbeat tone. I never would have guessed he expected anything but to be admitted.

After a long moment, a buzz sounded, and the gates swung open. Alex rolled up his window. "Well, I'll be damned. Never thought I would see the day those gates opened for me," he shot me a quick smile, put the car in gear, and accelerated up the drive to the gravel circle in front of the house, but instead of stopping, he took a lane that branched off to the right. He followed it around to the back of the house, where he turned the car, backing in so that the nose of the car faced the drive. "In case we need a quick get away."

"You're giving me a definite storming-the-castle vibe." We climbed out, and I slammed my door. "With all your drama, I'm almost expecting someone to come out of the house waving a gun at us."

"With Eve, I wouldn't be too sure. Of course, this is England, so she probably wouldn't have a gun. A crossbow or mace, possibly."

Alex led the way along a rock-paved path through a kitchen garden to a door at the back of the house. He tapped on the frame, and stepped back. We both expectantly watched the lace curtains that covered the window set in the door…and waited several minutes. Alex knocked again. "Perhaps the gate opening was a malfunction," I said.

Alex sent me a dark look. "Let's not be pessimistic." He leaned close to the window and squinted, trying to see through the fine holes in the lace. I turned and surveyed the back. Beyond the kitchen garden, the land spread in a wide green lawn with several interesting features. Thick hedges enclosed the lawn, and there was a wooden gate at one side with the hedge covering it in an arch as well as an oak tree with a rope swing hanging from one of the gnarled and twisted branches. "I can see why you'd want to use this place. I love the gate and the rope swing. And all that space outside the hedges, is it all property of Coventry House?"

"Yes, even into the woods in the distance."

A flash of movement on the other side of the door caught our attention. Through the distortions of the lace, I could see a shadowy figure moving slowly. A large hand, the joints as gnarled as the oak tree branches, parted the curtains, and we had a swift glimpse of a red cardigan over a flannel shirt, two bright if slightly rheumy blue eyes, and a thin shock of pure white hair. The curtain dropped and the door opened slowly.

Alex leaned forward, "Mr. Wallings, I'm Alex Norcutt. This is my colleague Kate Sharp. We're here—"

Mr. Wallings, his hold tight around the handles of a walker, was in the process of backing up so the door could open wider. He waved a hand, and I noticed a slight involuntary tremble before he gripped the walker again. "I know who you are. Movie people," he said with relish.

CHAPTER 12

*M*R. WALLINGS HAD INCHED BACKWARD, clearing a space for the door to swing wide. "Come in. Come in." He shifted the walker and shuffled down a hallway, calling over his shoulder. "Close the door behind you, if you don't mind."

We stepped inside and followed him down the hallway through a completely remodeled kitchen with stainless steel and bland cream countertops. Alex looked gutted. I sent him a sympathetic look. It could have been a kitchen in any house in any city in Middle America. Every trace of English Country House had been removed. Dishes were stacked in the sink and the island was cluttered with a crusty loaf of bread, a jar of spice, a bottle of olive oil, a mortar and pestle, and a food processor. It looked as if someone had stepped away and would be back in a few moments. I wondered if Eve Wallings was in the next room. If we ran into her, I had a feeling she wouldn't welcome us with open arms.

"Let's go in here," Mr. Wallings said as he moved laboriously through a dining room painted a pale gray, which retained its elegant lines with wainscoting and simple trim. A funky modern chandelier and padded, contemporary style seats surrounded the dark wood table and were at odds with the architecture of the room.

We moved across an airy hall with a wide staircase and through the open double doors to a drawing room. Mr. Wallings continued on into the room at his slow pace, but Alex and I both paused on the threshold and let out matching sighs of satisfaction, quickly cataloguing the highlights of the room: high ceilings, an Adam fireplace, and tall windows, which—as Austen would have described them—went all the way to the ground and gave a view of the green lawn. A set of French doors in the middle of the room opened onto a terrace.

I wasn't sure if the deep burgundy paint on the wall was Regency accurate, but it gave the room a warm feeling and contrasted nicely with the delicate stuccoed reliefs of garlands on the fireplace as well as the white wainscoting. A huge rug in the same rich burgundy tone with cream and blue accents covered the floor. The furniture was modern, a mix of squashy couches, deep chairs, and a hodgepodge of end tables that ran the gamut in style from delicate pie-edged to modern glass, but the room didn't seem disjointed or hectic. It felt cozy and lived-in, as if the room had been a place where families had gathered for hundreds of years.

I felt a little shiver that I sometimes got when I knew a location was 'it.' It was hard to describe, but despite the modern furniture and bold paint—even with the television on a cart tucked into one corner of the room—I knew that with some changes, this room would be the perfect setting for the Bennets. A glance at Alex confirmed that he felt the same way.

Mr. Wallings settled into a sturdy camelback chair upholstered in a cream and red plaid. He expertly swung the walker into an open space that was obviously reserved for it. On an end table at his side were a remote control, a box of tissues, several paperback books, a few prescription pill bottles, a stack of newspapers, and a mug filled with pens and pencils. His chair was positioned close enough to the windows that he had a wide view of the sweep of lawn down to the boundary hedge, and inside the room, his chair was angled so that the television faced him directly. "Oh, look, we've interrupted your lunch," I said, eyeing a tray with soup, bread, and a bowl of what looked like pudding or custard. "Should we come back another time?"

Out of the corner of my eye, I saw Alex send me a look that clearly said, *what are you thinking?* But I stayed focused on Mr. Wallings. No matter how hard it was to get in the house, interrupting Mr. Wallings' meal wasn't good form.

"I wasn't hungry. Can't stand that bland, tasteless stuff. Perhaps you could move the tray for me?"

"Of course." I moved it to a nearby table that Mr. Wallings indicated. As I set it down, a stack of papers slid to the floor. "So sorry." I crouched down. The papers had splayed out in a fan shape, and I shuffled bills, typed letters, a will, and newspapers folded open to the crossword together, then slapped an article torn from a magazine about an antique clock worth millions on top. A single paper had slid under a chair. I retrieved it, a note page covered with what looked like sketches for remodeling projects with bold slashed lines indicating new doorways or knocked-out walls. I added it to the other papers.

I looked around for a place to set down the bundle. Mr. Wallings held out his slightly trembling hand. "Don't worry. Need to do a good clear out of this room. I'll take them."

I handed the papers over and he shuffled through them. The vibration in his hands transferred to the pages, making them quiver. "What a mess." He shook his head as he rearranged the order of the papers. "These should be in my desk." He paused over the sketch, a displeased frown on his face then he put the pile down on the table beside him, causing the pencil jar to rock, but it didn't fall over. I took a seat beside Alex on a sagging cream-colored couch.

"Now, I suppose you'd like to look around, like the other chap? Evie's not here, but you don't need her," Mr. Wallings said. "I can help you—just like I did with him."

"So you spoke to Kevin Dunn?" Alex struggled to inch forward to the edge of the cushion, but the couch had attempted to swallow both of us and seemed to sag more as he struggled.

"Oh, yes. A fine fellow. Appreciated the old place, he did. I gave him the grand tour. He was interested in everything, said the library was perfect and the morning room and the bedrooms were just what he was looking for." He ran his gaze over the room, from the corners of the ceilings to the tall windows, but I had a feeling he was picturing the other parts of the house beyond the walls of the drawing room. He let out a dry wheezing sound. I realized Mr. Wallings was laughing. He gathered his breath and said, "I would let him make a movie here whether or not he liked the house. We need some shaking up here." The wheezing laugh came again. "Just to rile Evie, I would have said yes."

Alex and I exchanged another look. It's never good when the parties involved in a shoot are at odds with each other. Mr. Wallings picked up on the glance we shared and waved a shaky hand. "Don't worry. I am the sole owner, despite how Evie acts. I have the right—and authority—to grant use of my property to whomever I please."

"Does Eve know about your decision?"

His grin widened. "Not a clue." He was delighted with the idea of doing an end-run around Eve.

"You see, Evie enjoys managing people. She calls it taking care of people, which she's been doing for me." He rubbed his hand along his leg. "Broke my hip a couple of months back. She moved in. I had to have the help. Couldn't have made it without her, but now...I realize that I shouldn't have let her... immerse herself in my life. I had a touch of pneumonia at the time. I was weak as a kitten. But now that I've got my strength back, things are going to be different, starting with this movie. You can't be subtle with Evie. I need something big to show her things have changed." He clasped his hands together. "Now, let's get on to the paperwork."

Alex struggled forward and managed to balance on the edge of the cushion. "Mr. Dunn mentioned paperwork?"

"Yes. That's why you're here, isn't it? That and the photos? Dunn didn't have time to take any pictures inside. He said he had a plane to catch, but he'd send his associate along to photograph everything inside and bring the paperwork. Now, I want my solicitor to read over everything. You can leave it with me, and I'll get back to you."

"Mr. Wallings, I have to confess that this is all news to us," Alex said. "You see, I have some bad news about Mr. Dunn." Alex hesitated, clearly debating how much to tell him.

The gleeful excitement seeped out of Mr. Wallings' face. "Something has happened. Out with it, lad. I've heard my share of bad news."

"I'm sorry to tell you that Mr. Dunn has passed away."

Mr. Wallings reared back in his chair, his eyebrows raised. "But he was the picture of health."

"It wasn't like that," I said. "His car ran off the road into the river—"

I had to stop and clear my throat, but Mr. Wallings nodded, and murmured to himself, "So that's what Sherry and Evie were whispering about this morning. As if I have to be sheltered." He shook his head, then refocused on me. "I'm sorry to hear that. He seemed a good chap, and I was looking forward to meeting with him again. But seeing as it has happened, it doesn't change a thing. I'll still agree to the filming. Where are those papers?"

Alex wrestled his way out of the cushions and stood. He adjusted his jacket, resettling it on his shoulders, then moved to a straight-back chair set at a right angle to Mr. Wallings' chair. "I don't have any papers with me today. I'm going to be completely honest with you, Mr. Wallings. I had no idea that Mr. Dunn had even contacted you."

Mr. Wallings' rather significant eyebrows squished together. "Are you telling me you don't want to use Coventry House in your movie?"

"Oh, no, sir. Just the opposite." Alex looked toward me.

"It's perfect—exactly what we want," I said.

"So we're still on?" Mr. Wallings asked.

"Yes, if the project moves forward," I said. "With the death of Mr. Dunn, well…that could impact it."

"Might use someone else, you mean? For the—what did he call it? Location scouting?"

"Yes. That's the term," I said. "And that's the situation. We're unsure of what will happen."

"Bring me the papers anyway."

"I will."

I leaned forward, "Do you remember what time Kevin was here on Friday?"

"I suppose it was about two. He wanted to stay longer, but couldn't because of his flight." Mr. Wallings deftly swung the walker into place in front of his chair. "Let me show you around before you go. You can get your pictures now."

Alex gripped my wrist and pulled me free of the man-eating couch. I popped up and landed with my hand on his chest, so close that I could see a faint scar that ran along his hairline. I stepped back swiftly.

We photographed the drawing room and made notes, then set off at Mr. Wallings' slow pace, moving through the house, recording the morning room at the back of the house, papered in pale green striped silk, as well as a steamy conservatory and, finally, two bedrooms that were being used for storage. They were packed high with boxes, trunks, and odds and ends, like a coat stand, an old phonograph player, and stacks of dusty magazines. One room had an art deco bedroom set shoved to one side. Beyond the dresser with the smooth lines, I could make out another beautiful Regency-era fireplace. Delicately patterned wallpaper covered the walls in each room above the wainscoting, yellow stripes with vines in one and tiny blue and white flowers in the other. Once everything was cleared out, the rooms would be perfect. The light was good and the rooms were large enough to film in. I used a compass app on my phone and made notes in my Moleskine notebook. Alex took photos and measured the room, jotting down the numbers on his forearm. As we turned to follow Mr. Wallings down the hallway, I whispered to Alex. "This place is wonderful."

"I know. I can see why Mr. Dunn would jump at the chance to get it."

We returned to the main floor in a creaky elevator that was surely from the Victorian era, but the accordion grill was well-oiled and slid silently into place, and Mr. Wallings operated the circular crank without hesitation, so I assumed it was his normal mode of changing floors. Earlier, he'd sent Alex and me up the stairs and met us at the top after riding up in the elevator.

"This was a dumbwaiter," Mr. Wallings explained as he unlatched the grill.

I was pressed up against Alex's chest, a fact that seemed to take over my brain and made it hard for me to think of a reply. I managed to say, "How interesting." It seemed incredibly stuffy in the elevator, too, but it must have just been me, because when I tilted up my head, Alex didn't look uncomfortable. In fact, he had a teasing smile on his face as if he knew exactly how flustered I felt wedged against him.

We emerged from the elevator into an alcove in the hallway

between the dining room and the kitchen. I brushed my hair out of my face and tried to compose myself. What was wrong with me? I wasn't some starry-eyed tween with a crush. I was a grown woman in the middle of an important business meeting. "Thank you for meeting with us and showing us your home. It is lovely."

Mr. Wallings' face creased into a smile. "I certainly think so. I'm glad you agree." The smile slipped. "Again, I am sorry to hear about Mr. Dunn. Give my regards to the family."

"Thank you."

"Let's go out this way—you haven't seen this room yet." Mr. Wallings inched his way through the dining room and turned to another door near the drawing room. I think I let out an audible sigh when I crossed the threshold. The small room was a library, fitted out with floor-to-ceiling bookcases. Leather bound, gold-embossed tomes filled the shelves. Cushy armchairs were scattered across a navy Axminster carpet. A round table in glossy wood with books of maps, their page edges crinkled with age, filled the other side of the room. Scarlet drapes with gold trim bracketed the two sets of French doors, echoing the rich tones in the carpet and the bookbindings. Mr. Wallings moved to the French doors and exchanged his walker for a cane that was positioned against the wall near the door.

We followed him out onto a slate terrace that ran the length of the house. Large pots positioned along the terrace held evergreen bushes trimmed into tall cone shapes, effectively enclosing the space. A set of shallow steps led to a gravel path lined with boxwood hedges. A fountain, which was dry and only had a few brown leaves in it, was positioned in the center of the garden. One side of the stairs had been fitted with a wooden ramp, and Mr. Wallings made his way easily down the slight slope to the gravel.

The house seemed well modified for him, and I was a little

surprised that Eve had been able to completely cut off communication between Alex and Mr. Wallings. But then again, maybe he only moved easily on his own property. I supposed getting into the village would be another matter. I wondered if he was able to drive.

I was about to ask how often he visited the village when I heard the sound of feet crunching across the gravel. We all turned in the direction of the sound, the back corner of the house. Eve appeared, walking alongside a young man who pushed a wheelbarrow containing some of the large, flat stones I'd seen so often in the boundary walls. A shapeless canvas hat with a wide brim shaded Eve's eyes. She wore a tan windbreaker over a black sweater and jeans, which were tucked into knee-high rubber boots. She held a pair of work gloves in one hand.

She had been moving slowly and a bit wearily, but the moment she spotted us, her shoulders snapped back, and she shot forward as if she'd had an electric shock.

"Uncle Edwin, where is your coat? You shouldn't be outside without it. The wind—"

He cut her off. "It's mild enough here in the garden."

She threw a quick, searing glance at Alex and me. The words, "I'll deal with you in a moment," weren't spoken aloud, but they didn't need to be. Her look said it all. The young man with the wheelbarrow swerved, taking a course that kept him on the outskirts of the garden. He whipped through the exterior plantings and disappeared behind a tall hedge.

"And you're using your cane," Eve said, her tone exasperated. "You know what the doctor said. You're to use the walker *at all times.* Where is Sherry? She's supposed to be with you."

"School called. Her son was sick. I told her to go on."

Eve glanced briefly at the sky and muttered, "Going off and leaving him alone. What was she thinking? Let's get you back inside," Eve's voice changed abruptly to fake brightness, the sort of tone that teachers use with cranky preschoolers. "Watch that slope into the house. It can be tricky." Eve moved a half a step toward the house, but Mr. Wallings pointed his toes toward the center of the garden where several chairs ranged around the fountain. "None of your bills, and papers, and signatures, today, Evie. I fancy a bit of time in the sun." He set off at his slow pace. Eve's face pinched and flushed.

"Maybe we should be going." I took a step backward. "We can see ourselves out."

Eve hissed, "Yes, leave. And if I ever see you again on this property—"

"Evie!" Mr. Wallings called sharply. "Please remember that these people are my guests." He'd settled into one of the chairs, his face turned up to the sun. His hands rested on the cane, which he'd laid across the arms of the chair.

Eve took a deep breath and then smoothed her hands over the windbreaker, her gaze focused somewhere beyond Alex and me. "Of course." Her voice was stilted. "I apologize. You see, my main concern is for my uncle. He has to be very careful."

"I'm just old, Evie," Mr. Wallings interjected, "not deathly ill."

The pink patches on Eve's cheeks brightened.

Mr. Wallings called out, "You should get to know these people, Evie. We'll be seeing quite a lot of them in the future. They will be filming here."

"What?" Eve turned back to Mr. Wallings, a disapproving glare on her face. "That's not a good idea—"

Mr. Wallings cut her off. "It's settled, Evie. It will happen."

Alex said, "I'm sure there are things you need to discuss. We were just leaving."

"It's settled. There's nothing to discuss," Mr. Wallings said. "Look forward to seeing you both in a few days—next Monday, shall we say?"

"Monday, then," Alex said. "Good to see you again, Ms. Wallings. No need to see us out."

"No, I'll come with you," Eve said firmly and led the way to a path that circled around the front of the house.

Alex said, "I parked around the side."

She nodded, and we trooped on in a tense, silent bubble. When we reached Alex's car, she said, "I know you don't understand, Mr. Norcutt, but Uncle Edwin needs rest and quiet. No excitement. He's probably already nodding off out there in the garden—he always has a nap after lunch. Now Jacob will have to help him inside."

"Does he have some sort of heart or nerve problem?" Alex opened his door and rested his arm on it. "I thought he was recovering from a broken hip and pneumonia."

"His medical diagnosis is not your concern. This is *not* a viable location for you to use. I won't stand for it."

"It's his property," Alex said, his voice quiet. "If he wants to allow us to use Coventry House...then it's his prerogative."

Alex was on the other side of the car from Eve. She stepped closer, and I could see the quick rise and fall of her chest. "He doesn't know what is good for him. That's why I am here—to take care of him. And if you think you can get around me, you're wrong. I won't allow him to be upset."

"He didn't seem to be upset at the idea of filming," I said. "In fact, it seemed to energize him."

Eve's attention had been focused on Alex, but at my words, her gaze pierced me. "You think you can waltz in here from Los Angeles—oh yes, I heard about you—and charm him, but you'll not get past me. I will stop this foolishness."

I knew when to cut my losses. I didn't think there was a thing we could say to change Eve's mind or convince her to reconsider. I opened the car door, which forced her to step back. Alex didn't follow my lead. Instead of slipping into the car as I did, he said, "I'm afraid that's not your call, Ms. Wallings. We'll be in touch."

Alex dropped into the driver's seat and started the car. Eve stood, watching us until a twist in the drive took us out of sight.

Alex downshifted as we neared the gates, which were swinging open automatically as we approached. "I shouldn't have said that."

"I don't think there's anything you could have said to smooth things over."

"Nevertheless, that parting gouge was uncalled for. It's never smart to intentionally alienate clients."

"I think she was already alienated."

Alex snorted as he navigated through the gates, then turned onto the road after a brief pause. "Especially with me."

I gripped the door handle, instinctively bracing for an accident because I felt as if we were pulling into the wrong lane. Even after driving myself and being in England for a couple of days, driving on the left side of the road still felt wrong. "She didn't exactly embrace me either."

"Only because you were with me. You're tainted by association."

"I think the L.A./Hollywood connection did the tainting."

"There is that, too."

"I don't know if it's worth it—to pursue Coventry House. There's a lot of baggage there," I said.

"I know," Alex said. The road had curved back on itself, and we had a glimpse of Coventry House's gables above the trees.

I sighed. "Too bad it's so exactly right."

"It may all come to nothing, in the end. Especially if the whole project folds."

We drove in silence for a few minutes, then the arched stone bridge came into view, and all thoughts of Coventry

House fell away. I caught Alex's sleeve. "Let's stop here. Do you mind?"

He shook his head and slowed the car, letting it roll to a stop in the clearing near the steep plunge down to the water. I got out and moved to the edge. Alex followed me. Out of the corner of my eye, a dark shape moved, blending in with the mix of trees that rimmed the small open area. "Someone else is here."

CHAPTER 13

"IT'S A PUBLIC PLACE," ALEX said. "Nothing to be alarmed at."

"I know, but there was something about the way the person moved. It was sneaky, as if they didn't want to be seen." I squinted into the shadows under the trees, but nothing moved.

"Probably a rambler," Alex said.

"Then why aren't they rambling? There's definitely someone there—not moving. They're hiding," I said, my gaze caught on a patch of something shining red-gold in a narrow shaft of sunlight that had penetrated through the tree canopy. "We know you're there. You can come out," I called.

"Oh, all right." It was a female voice with a British accent. Becca stepped from behind a tree trunk. "I always was rubbish at any sort of Girl Guide thing—anything to do with the outdoors, really." As she moved up the little path to the clearing, Alex met her and extended his hand, pulling her up the last foot. "Thank you. Such strength." She brushed her hand along Alex's bicep.

Alex took a step back, but she moved with him, linking her

fingers together around his arm. "So what are you two doing? Taking in a bit of the local scenery? Oh! Are you scouting this location? It would be wonderful for Elizabeth and Mr. Darcy's stroll, wouldn't it?"

"No. We're not," I said. "Why are you here?" Normally, I'd go out of my way to keep the owner of a potential location happy, but I was tired of her affected manner, and I had that same feeling I'd had earlier in the day, that she was keeping something back.

"Oh, strolling. A, um, ramble, really."

I crossed my arms. "You just said you don't like the outdoors. I think the only touring of the countryside that you do is from the driver's seat of your SUV."

Becca didn't seem to know what to do when flirting and/or teasing wasn't the order of the day. She laughed, but it sounded forced. "What do you mean? I adore walks. I walk *all* the time. Just like dear Lizzy in *Pride and Prejudice.*"

"Interesting that you were 'walking' here in the exact spot where Kevin's car went in the water. You know something about that day—something that you didn't mention earlier, don't you? You were going to say something when we told you about Kevin's death, but you stopped yourself."

"That's absurd."

"You're overdoing the outraged tone," I said. "Makes you seem even less believable."

"Did you and Kevin talk about something else that you didn't tell us about?"

She relaxed, and her voice sounded completely natural when she said, "No, of course not."

"Did you see him again? Later?" Her eyes widened a touch, and I knew I was right. "That's it. You saw him. It was here, right? It had to be here. Why else would you be here and not want anyone to see you? Why would you hide when we arrived?"

"Yes, I did see him again." Becca's voice was petulant. "He couldn't drop Grove Cottage. I had to make him see that."

I'd been so focused on her face, which clearly showed that I was right—she had kept something back—that I didn't notice Alex's expression until that moment. He shook his head, a warning look on his face. I backed up a step, bumped into his car, realizing the implications of Becca's statement. She was here with Kevin, near the place his body had been found. Being here alone in the quiet countryside with Becca and making accusations—not the smartest moves I'd ever made, I belatedly realized. Beyond Alex and Becca, the water streamed away to the area where Kevin had been found. If Becca found Kevin here and was angry with him, had she pushed him? He could have slipped, perhaps hit his head on the rocks that bulged out from the bank and been swept downstream.

"Oh, don't look at me like that," Becca said impatiently. "I didn't do anything to him. Well, not really."

I licked my lips as I moved my hand along the car door, searching for the handle. Not that it would do me much good to get the door open. I didn't have the car keys. "Why don't you tell us what happened?"

Alex said, "I think this is a conversation you need to have with the investigating officer, Quimby."

Becca rolled her eyes. "Don't be so dramatic. Nothing happened. We talked. I left. That was it."

"How did you find him?" Alex had managed to untangle his arm from her hand and had moved slightly so that the three of us were in a triangle formation with me at the car, Alex to my right with his back to the water, and Becca to his right with her back to the woods.

She fiddled with the threads where her coat was missing a button. "I went to the inn, but his car wasn't there, so I drove around a bit, looking for him. He wasn't at Coventry House, so I took this road. I saw his car pulled over here." She nodded at

Alex's car. "He'd had a flat and had changed the tire. I stopped. We chatted."

"Did you convince him to change his mind?" I asked.

"No." Her lips puckered into a pout. "He was set on Coventry House, but he said you still might use Grove Cottage for Lucas Lodge." You'd have thought Lucas Lodge was the equivalent of dog poop from her tone.

"So your house was still under consideration, then."

"Tourists don't travel hundreds or thousands of miles to see Lucas Lodge," she said scathingly. "No, I told him I wouldn't let him back out. He said Grove Cottage would be Longbourn, and it will be. I told him I was on my way to personally visit my solicitor in London the next day."

"What did he say?" Alex asked.

"He laughed." A flush of red suffused her cheekbones. "Said it didn't matter. That there hadn't been a verbal agreement." She straightened the hem of her hip-length trench coat and squared her shoulders. "I told him we'd see about that, and I— well—I left."

There was that hesitation again, that fractional tick in her speech that betrayed her. "You left at that moment?"

"Yes," she said quickly.

"Then why come back here today after you got the news that Kevin had died? And why sneak around and hide from us when we arrived?" I said slowly, remembering Quimby's questions, his very specific questions. "You're afraid that you left something here."

I pushed off from the car and closed the distance between Becca and me. "That's a Burberry trench coat, isn't it?" I asked as I fingered one of the buttons near the lapel. "Yes, it is. I can tell because the brand name is stamped into each button. That's what you're looking for, your lost button." I pointed to the threads that dangled where a button was missing.

"What are you talking about? Who cares if I lost a button?"

"DCI Quimby cares." I pulled my cell phone out of my pocket. "You're right, Alex, this is a conversation for Quimby."

"No, wait," Becca lunged for my phone, but Alex stepped between us, knocking her hand away.

"Let her make the call."

"No, you don't understand." Becca smiled up at him through her false eyelashes. "Let me explain. It's not what you think."

"I thought you already explained." I'd moved several steps back and was scrolling through my recent call list. I found the number, but then glanced up at Alex. "No service."

"I'll try." Alex checked his phone, moved a few steps in one direction, then shifted to the opposite direction.

"So, I left out a detail or two—that's not a crime," Becca said. "Let me tell you what happened. You'll see there's no need to call anyone official. Everything I said before is true. Kevin was here; we talked. I was fiddling with that idiotic loose button when he laughed at me. It made me so mad. The button came off in my hand, and I dropped it. At the time, I didn't stop to look for it. When you told me what had happened to Kevin, I remembered about the button. Naturally, I don't want to be involved in a police investigation—so common, you know." She sighed, clearly exasperated. "I've searched everywhere." She waved her arm, taking in the clearing, the woods, the drop to the water.

"Oh, I think it was here, but I bet it is evidence now. Quimby asked me specifically if I owned a brown Burberry trench coat."

"That's not good," she said, then her face brightened. "But lots of people have trench coats."

"I think the pool of people who can pay over a thousand dollars for a trench coat is probably pretty small, especially in a town the size of Nether Woodsmoor."

Alex raised his eyebrows, and I said, "We used some on a commercial shoot once. Inventory lists."

"Ah."

"This is all Kevin's fault," Becca said. "If he hadn't laughed at me—hadn't made me mad—I wouldn't have pushed his car into the river."

CHAPTER 14

"YOU KNOW, THIS HAS BEEN really interesting, Mrs. Ford, but we have an appointment back in Nether Woodsmoor," Alex said.

Thoughts skittered around my mind, the primary one being I didn't want to be in this out-of-the-way bit of countryside with Becca. I wanted people and movement around me, not just the low murmur of flowing water and the wind whispering through the treetops. A few cars had passed on the road while we talked, but it was quiet now.

Becca threw up her hands, palms out. "I should never have said that—or said it that way. It isn't what you think. I told you, nothing happened."

"Except you pushed Kevin's car into the river. I think that's something." The words popped out, and I immediately wished I could take them back. *Don't goad the woman who'd just admitted shoving a dead man's car into the river. Just leave.* "Never mind," I said quickly as I opened the car door, "Alex is right. I'd forgotten all about that appointment. We should go."

"But Mr. Dunn wasn't in the car." Becca grabbed the car door, holding it open. "I know it sounds rather bad, but he wasn't in it. And it's not as if I *rammed* it. I was a tad upset and pressed the accelerator a hair too much. I didn't realize how close I was to his car. My bumper barely grazed his. It only pushed it forward an inch or so, but with all the rain, the ground must have been very soft near the edge of the water." She raised her eyebrows, a meaningful look on her face. "He shouldn't have parked so close to the edge, you know. It all happened so fast. The car went right over the edge. There was nothing we could do to stop it." Despite the urge to leave, I was fascinated with Becca's animated face. She likes this, I realized, being the center of attention. She enjoyed telling her story in the most dramatic way possible.

She thrust her hands into her pockets. "And it's not as if it was even his own car. It was a hire, for heaven's sake. He wouldn't even have had to pay for it."

It was such an idiotic statement that I think I actually gaped at her with my mouth open for a moment.

"I'm sure he had full coverage," Becca added.

The car rental issue and who would pay for the car didn't matter now, so I swept those thoughts aside. "So what happened next?"

"I left."

"You *left?*"

"Yes, he was fine." Her voice was sharp with impatience. "I *told* you that. He was on the bank, but not near the car when it went in. He was fine. Absolutely fine."

"So let me get this straight," I said. "You not only left the scene of an accident, you also left Kevin out here with no transportation?"

"Yes. It's not that far from the village, and it wasn't raining hard. Only drizzling. Light drizzle, in fact. But you're missing the main point—he was alive when I left."

I rubbed my forehead, too astounded at her attitude to come up with a reply.

Alex had been waving his phone around, looking for a signal. "Ah, here we go," he said. Before he could dial, his phone rang. "Detective Sergeant Olney, thank you for returning my call. Yes, we—that is Ms. Sharp and I have—have some information for you. You're in Nether Woodsmoor now? That is fortunate. Then perhaps you could meet us at the bridge? That's where we are now...Yes, that bridge. Becca Ford is here too, looking for a button she lost...that's what I said, a button. A Burberry button, to be exact. Yes, she has additional information for you as well. Excellent."

At the beginning of the call, Becca had looked wary. By the end she was glowering at him, her face tight and angry.

Alex ended the call. "He'll be along shortly."

"I THINK I got off pretty easily with Olney," I said. Alex and I were at the White Duck having dinner. I ate the last golden fry —or chip, as Alex had informed me I should refer to them.

"Becca's news did overshadow yours," he said.

I'd confessed all about the camera memory card. Olney had talked to us first and then said we could leave. When we left the bridge, he was still asking Becca questions. "Pushing someone's car into the river is a bit more dramatic than 'I found a memory card with some pictures.'"

Alex put down his pint of beer and smiled. "True, but both were valuable bits of news."

"Oh, I know. And I'm not upset at all to have Becca in the police spotlight. I'm glad she's there instead of me."

"Yes, I'd venture to say she enjoys the spotlight."

As soon as Alex had ended his call with Olney, Becca had threatened to leave so she could call her lawyer. But leaving would have involved walking over the trails back to her house. The lack of transportation combined with the fact that Olney looked as if he could pose on a law enforcement beefcake calendar meant that Becca was retelling her version of events, relishing Olney's undivided attention.

I pushed away the empty plate that contained only crumbs from my fish and chips. "Do you think she's telling the truth? That Kevin really was okay when she left?"

"I can't imagine her making up the story."

"And hurting Kevin might take her further away from her goal of having Grove Cottage used in the production," I said. "Is it possible she didn't realize that? That she thought killing him would make it easier to get her home used?"

Alex shrugged. "Becca isn't one to think deeply about things."

"You think she was angry and acted on that emotion impulsively? That would make it a crime of passion." I paused a moment, considering it, then said, "Yes, I can totally see that happening."

Alex nodded, "It could have happened that way, but then why would she admit to being at the river and pushing Kevin's car into the water? It would be better to deny everything or clam up completely until the police actually linked her to the scene."

"Not talking doesn't seem to be her strong suit," I said.

"That's true." Alex wiped his hands on his napkin and pushed his plate away. "As astounding as Becca's explanation was, I'm leaning toward believing her. At least the bare bones of her story. Now, whether it really was an accidental graze of her car bumper—I'm not so sure."

I nodded. "I can imagine her anger flaring up and her flooring it. Her mood changes are...mercurial."

"That's putting it mildly. Of course, if everything goes her way, then she's fine."

"She's the type of woman who always has *something* that doesn't go her way."

Alex raised his beer in agreement. "You said that, not me."

"I keep thinking about Kevin alone out there. If only he'd called someone."

"Cell phone coverage is spotty along there. You saw how hard it was for me to find a signal, and he probably didn't have True Call, best service of the Midlands. Or, maybe his phone was dead."

"That is a definite possibility. He was always running the battery down and forgetting to charge it at night," I said. "Becca's news may explain why his car was in the water, but we still don't know what happened to him, how he ended up in the water downstream. And it doesn't explain his broken leg or the head injury either. The drop to the water isn't a cliff. It's not like he'd have multiple impacts if he fell or was pushed. He'd probably hit once, if that, then be in the water." My stomach turned as I pictured it, and wished I hadn't eaten such a heavy, greasy meal.

Alex dipped his head to look at my downturned face. "You look a little pale. Feeling okay?"

"Thinking about him in the water…it bothers me."

"Yeah, me too." After a few beats of silence, Alex said, "You know, I don't know what your favorite Jane Austen book is. We've already covered mine."

I couldn't help but smile. "You've only read one."

"There you go. My favorite. Which is yours? You were an English grad student, so it's practically required, right?"

"Yes, mandatory for admission to the program. I have a special place in my heart for *Northanger Abbey*, but it's not my absolute favorite."

"You say that almost reluctantly."

"Northanger Abbey is sort of the redheaded stepchild of Austen's books. It's often considered a bridge book between her juvenilia and her 'adult' books, but I love the teasing banter between Catherine and Mr. Tilney and the discussion of novels and books and reading. My all-time favorite is quite run-of-the-mill. It's *Pride and Prejudice*, of course."

"And why is that?"

"It's brilliant. Brilliantly written. The plot, the dialogue, the characters. Austen really was a genius." I leaned back in my chair. "I planned to write my dissertation on it."

"What about?"

"I wanted to explore Austen's contrast of appearance versus reality. Judgments are made about a character based on a person's appearance and manners, but often those judgments are completely wrong."

"Hmm...yes, like Wickham."

"Exactly. He's accepted because he's handsome, charming, and has a good address, but inside he's a lazy, selfish man willing to ruin a young woman's reputation to further his own goals. Mr. Darcy is his foil. Outwardly perceived to be cold and proud, but inwardly he is honorable and responsible. The surface, the outer appearance, is often different from the interior, the heart," I said, and I couldn't help but wonder if someone in Nether Woodsmoor had put up an excellent front to mask the evil inside them. Becca could have killed Kevin, but if she was telling the truth and Kevin was alive when she left that meant the murderer was still out there.

I glanced at Alex. His face was serious, and I wondered if his thoughts were running along the same lines as mine. "This conversation is way too deep—and probably too boring," I said. "You're nice to indulge an English lit major and let me run on."

Alex's phone, which was on the table between us, rang. A picture of a daisy appeared on the screen above the name Grace.

Alex said, "Sorry, I've got to take this." A burst of laughter sounded from a table behind us, and he put his hand over his other ear. He spoke a few words, then said, "Hold on a moment." He made an apologetic face and stepped outside.

Louise cleared the empty plates, and I told myself that it was perfectly fine that Alex had gotten a call from someone named Grace, and that I hadn't felt a small flare of...jealousy? No, it couldn't be that. I barely knew Alex. I was irritated, nothing more, at the interruption. That was it. That had to be it. He was a colleague.

A colleague who happened to be very easy on the eyes, an internal voice whispered. And extremely nice. He'd brought me coffee and spent his time shuttling me around the countryside. I firmly squashed that internal voice. *Colleague*, I reminded myself. It was best to keep things professional.

Alex returned, but didn't take his seat again. "I have to go. If you're going to the inn, I'll walk you back."

I hesitated.

"Or, if you're staying here, I'll shove off."

The pub was getting more crowded by the minute. I didn't really want to stick around. "No, I'm ready."

Twilight filled the sky with a ruddy glow, backlighting the stone buildings. The air was sharp and even cold. I shoved my hands in the pockets of my peacoat, and we paced along silently, but it wasn't the comfortable quiet of earlier in the day. Now it seemed strained—at least it did to me. Alex didn't offer an explanation of who Grace was, and I didn't ask. She could be a friend or a business contact. Or a girlfriend, whispered the little voice. *Okay, yes, a girlfriend. That was a possibility, too.* That thought irritated me. I didn't want to examine why.

We reached the inn and crossed the courtyard. Alex opened the door and stepped into the entrance area, but kept his hand on the door. "About tomorrow...I won't be around. I have to go to Sheffield."

"Yes, of course. You've already taken more time with me than you should have. You need to keep up your business."

"Oh, you know how this business is. It comes in fits and starts, with dry spells in between."

"Yes. Thanks for dinner." I reached for my wallet. "I should pay you back for mine." He'd ordered our food at the bar and paid for it before I had a chance to offer.

"No, don't worry about it. You can get it next time." He pushed open the door.

I turned to climb the stairs slowly, feeling just the tiniest bit blue. Jet-lag, probably. Yes, I decided, picking up my pace, that was it. An eight-hour time change does make you draggy. A good night's sleep was all I needed.

UNFORTUNATELY, a good night's sleep wasn't what I got. I tossed and turned, sleeping fitfully for a few hours, then came awake and stared at the ceiling for what felt like hours. My internal clock was good and messed up. Finally, as dawn began to filter through the curtains, I dropped off into a deep sleep. I woke several hours later and groped for my phone. Ten-thirty. I scrubbed my hand across my face, thinking that a late morning nap was not the best cure for jet-lag. I felt better after a shower. Henry, who was shutting down the breakfast service, brought me a cup of coffee and some crumpets. I sat down in the empty restaurant to use the inn's free Wi-Fi.

I'd brought my personal cell phone as well as the burner phone Marci had given me. While I waited for my email to load, I checked both phones. I hoped the burner phone would have a message from Quimby. The revelations about Becca had to have steered the investigation toward her, but the only message I had was from DS Olney, informing me that the inquest would be held next week. The call had come in while I was showering, and I wished I had been able to speak to him. Did the scheduling of the inquest mean that Becca was the murderer, or was scheduling the date unrelated to the new information around Becca? I returned the call, but was only able to leave a voicemail with my questions. Almost immediately, a text came back from Olney stating that he couldn't release any information about the case.

I sighed and moved on to scanning the messages on my personal phone. A text message from Terrance headed the list. I'd called him yesterday and left him a voicemail telling him about Kevin's death. I frowned as I opened the text. I'd expected him to call back, not text.

Sorry to hear about Kevin. That's rough. Call me when you're back.

That's rough? That was his idea of comfort and support? I deleted the text, disappointed that he hadn't even felt the need to call me. My mother had been right about my "relationship" with Terrance, it seemed. It wasn't a relationship at all. We were just two people who exchanged a lot of texts and occasionally met for a meal. I realized that I wasn't even that sad. I didn't feel even the tiniest urge to indulge in my two break-up comfort foods, chocolate or fettuccine alfredo.

I straightened my shoulders and refocused on my texts. There would be time to sort out my love life later—or just get a love life. I dealt quickly with texts from a few friends and several from my mom, but paused over the last text from Janie, a production manager I'd worked with on a shoot last year. Can you send me Zara's new phone number? Saw her in the international terminal at JFK last week. Couldn't get through security fast enough to catch her.

I texted back Zara's current phone number with a frown. Surely Janie was mistaken. Zara had said she was in Chicago sorting out some legal stuff with her ex-husband.

My email finally loaded, and I saw a message from Marci had come in overnight. She still hadn't heard back from Mr. O'Leery.

To see if there were any hints or rumors about the future of the *P & P* project, I did an Internet search. A couple of tribute pieces in industry news sources topped the results, mostly recaps of Kevin's career—tame stuff compared to the guesswork going on in the Internet forums, which abounded with speculation about what had happened. The secrecy of the scouting trip had only fueled the guesswork. Theories ranged from Kevin's participation in some unknown super-secret project of Mr. O'Leery's to the more sordid hints that Kevin was involved in an affair.

As I scrolled through the list of threads that mentioned Kevin's name on one Internet forum, I stopped on one titled, "Kevin Dunn's Death: *Cui bono?*" I clicked the link and read the first post. "All this speculation about hush-hush projects is just fodder to obscure the obvious. Who benefits from Kevin Dunn's death? The answer is easy—his employees. One of the women in his office will step into his shoes, take over his clients, and be sitting pretty in a few months."

Had Quimby seen this? Was this post the reason he'd questioned me so closely about taking over Kevin's business? Did the police search Internet forums? It didn't seem outside the realm of possibility, especially with all the government surveillance that went on now. A modern police investigation probably included a web search.

I quickly scrolled through the replies, which accused the original poster of doing nothing more than trotting out a new conspiracy theory. Other posts agreed that the theory was possible. The original poster chimed in again. "Interesting tidbit. Just heard that one of the employees, Kate Sharp, arrived in England after he disappeared. Anyone know anything about her? Is she the type to take a short cut and help herself get to the top?"

Stunned and sickened, I skimmed through the rest of the comments, but the thread took a detour at that point and people began to discuss what was okay and not okay in going after jobs in the entertainment industry. The consensus seemed to be that it was so hard to get a foot in the door that a little sneaky manipulation was fine. The last post read, "Yeah, sure, I understand times are tough and getting a start or a leg up in this business is hard, but murder? That's over the line."

I wanted to close my laptop and go...wash my hands or something. I felt slimy. I couldn't believe that anyone would think I was out to take Kevin's place and that I'd resort to murder to achieve that goal. Another piece of advice from Kevin flitted through my mind: "Forewarned is forearmed. Find out everything you can—even the bad stuff. It'll help you in the end."

I blew out a deep breath and went back to the top of the thread. The original poster's screen name was "FilmGeek27," and had a very thin profile. No posts prior to the post about me and only a few more comments made that same day. I searched a few more forums and found one other mention of my name, with the same accusations, this time from "CinemaGuru," which again was a recently created profile with only a smattering of posts on the day my name was brought up and then nothing since then.

I slapped the laptop closed and dropped it off in my room, then picked up my camera and tote bag and went outside. I needed a good brisk walk to clear my head. Steel-gray clouds hung low and a strong, cold breeze whipped across my face, making my eyes water, but I pressed on, up the steep climb to the top of Strange Hill. The gloomy, wild weather was a match for my mood. As I paused at the top, catching my breath and taking in the view of Grove Cottage, I felt better after the exercise. The little valley was quiet except for the tree branches, which were shaking in the wind, and a few cars moving along the roads. One of them was a small red car, and I squinted, trying to see if it was Alex, but then a big dog popped up through the open passenger window and turned its nose into the wind...so probably not Alex.

I pulled my camera out of my tote bag and snapped some pictures of the village as well as a few close-ups of ivy climbing up the stone wall. The village had too many present-day features like street signs and electric street lights, not to mention pavement. We couldn't use it in the production, but I liked the rows of golden stone cottages. These photos would be just for me.

I contemplated the trail that the two ramblers had taken, considering whether or not I should continue my walk, but decided I should return to the village. Hiking a trail sounded like a nice way to spend the morning, even in the blustery weather, but it wouldn't bring any answers about what had happened to Kevin. Instead of returning to the inn, I went to the pub for lunch, hoping I could pick up some news or even rumors about the investigation.

They had classic pub grub like fish and chips and cottage pie, which sounded good, but it was described as a serving for two. For a second, I wished Alex was with me, so we could split it, but I squashed the thought and ordered a chicken and bacon sandwich from the more contemporary section of the menu. I didn't see Louise. A guy who I guessed was in his mid-twenties with blue eyes, an angular face, and a fringe of black hair dipping over his eyes brought my food. He disappeared, so there was no opportunity to chat with him, and the few other patrons in the pub were absorbed in their own meals and didn't look as if they wanted to chat with a stranger. My food was delicious and as I devoured it, I pulled out my Moleskine notebook. If I couldn't find someone to talk to, I could at least get my thoughts down on paper.

I printed the word, "Possibilities," across the top of a clean page. "Suspects" seemed too presumptuous. I wasn't a detective, but there was value in getting everything down on paper. Managing projects had taught me that.

I wrote for a few minutes, then read over my list.

. . .

1. Frank Revel—Argued publicly with Kevin and had a falling out with him years ago, but would he attack Kevin after fifteen years?

2. Becca Ford—Determined that Grove Cottage will be Longbourn. Admits to being near the place where Kevin's body was found and to pushing his car into the river. Was Kevin really alive when she left? Mercurial mood changes. Crime of passion?

3. Eve Wallings—Opposed to us using Coventry House. Very intense in her protection of her uncle. Would she kill Kevin, thinking that would keep us out of Coventry House?

4. Random act of violence?

5. Unknown person with unknown motive?

I REVIEWED THE LIST, then drew a line through Eve's name. Eve didn't know about Kevin's visit to Coventry House until Mr. Wallings told her in the garden.

I sighed and tilted my head to one side as I rubbed my neck. I had no real answers and too many question marks on my list. I heard my name and looked up to see Beatrice striding toward me. I quickly closed the notebook.

"Kate, just the person I need. We were in the process of painting when Kevin came out with Mr. Dunn and his group. Alex had mentioned that they would like some photos of the drawing room after the scaffolds were down and the curtains had been rehung, something about using it as the interior for Netherfield, I think he said. But perhaps I was wrong? Don't they want Parkview Hall for Pemberley?"

"Yes, but they were also considering using a few of the rooms for the interior scenes for Netherfield. Cost savings you know."

"I see. Makes perfect sense. I wondered if it would be possible for him to come take the photos today? I know it's short notice, but we have our soft opening for the season tomorrow. I hope you'll come. Free admission for everyone from the village before our official opening next weekend."

"I'd love to come."

"Glad to hear it. Now, will you be in touch with Alex today about the photos or should I call him?"

"I don't think he'll be able to do it. He has an appointment this morning, but I could do it. In fact, I could come over now."

"That would work." The young man with the black hair brought Beatrice a Styrofoam to-go box in a plastic bag. "I'm dropping this off for Edwin on the way, so if you don't mind a stop, you can ride with me."

"Much safer than me driving it on my own," I said.

CHAPTER 15

*B*EATRICE WAS DRIVING THE BEAT-up Range Rover again. The clouds had broken up and patches of bright sunlight shone through the drifts of clouds. Beatrice slipped on a pair of sunglasses, and I wished I had some as well. As we climbed into Beatrice's car, a tall woman driving a small blue hatchback slowed as she came even with the Range Rover and rolled down her window. "Hello, Beatrice."

"Oh, hello, Celia. Any luck with the clothing store in Brunner's Hill?"

She shook her head.

"I'm sorry," Beatrice said. "I'm sure something will turn up soon. I'll call you if I hear of anything."

"Perhaps you might need an extra pair of hands at the opening?"

"Yes, I think we might. Can you be there about seven?"

"Of course." The woman waved, a relieved look on her face.

Beatrice slammed her door. "She'll be there at six-thirty. Most dependable, competent woman in Nether Woodsmoor," Beatrice pulled onto the road and floored the accelerator. "Still don't understand why Eve let her go."

153

I braced a hand against the door as Beatrice took a sweeping curve like she was in the Monaco Grand Prix. When Beatrice drove me from Parkview Hall to the bridge, I'd assumed she drove quickly because of the unusual circumstances—submerged car and emergency responders on the way, but judging by the way we were flying through the countryside, I decided that it was probably her normal driving style.

"So she worked at Coventry House?" I asked, trying not to think about how fast the hedges were flicking by the window.

"Oh, yes. Eve let Celia go." Beatrice shook her head. "No reason for it that I could see. Eve is an excellent household manager, but I don't understand that decision at all. She hired that rather slatternly Sherry, who worked at the inn. She can cook—I will allow that, but Doug confided in me he was quite glad to see her go. I'd take Celia in a second if we had an opening, but all our positions are filled." Beatrice sighed and ran her hands loosely along the sides of the steering wheel. "I shouldn't gossip, but it's hard not to about curious things. Here we are." She stomped on the brakes and our seatbelts got a workout as we waited for the gates at Coventry House to open.

We sailed up the drive and around to the back of the house. She threw the car in park and picked up the plastic bag.

"I'll wait here," I said. "I don't think Eve will be glad to see me."

Beatrice paused with the door half open. "So what I heard last week is true, that Grove Cottage is no longer slated to be Longbourn and Coventry House is?"

"Looks that way. If the production goes forward."

"That will have Becca behaving rather like Mrs. Bennet, I expect."

I couldn't help but laugh. "Unfortunately, she's bent on consulting her lawyer, not a doctor."

"I'm sure it will work out. Becca's the type to throw a huge fuss, but like Mrs. Bennet, she'll come around in the end and declare the whole thing was her idea—that she refused to give permission for you to use Grove Cottage or some such nonsense."

"That would be an improvement over the way things are now. Becca is not happy with me, and I'm in Eve's black books, too, so I'll stay here."

"You should come inside. If Edwin's given you permission to use his house, then Eve has to deal with it. She's gotten far too used to ordering him around. I think it's a good thing actually, him standing up to her."

I reached for the door handle. "I suppose it wouldn't hurt to test the waters and see what the response is."

When we reached the back door Beatrice didn't knock, just opened it and called out. We entered the empty kitchen where the odor of cigarette smoke was strong. "Hmm...appears Sherry was in here recently," Beatrice said as she led the way by the island, which was again covered. A food processor stood beside a mortar and pestle along with several dirty bowls and a mix of eggs, spice jars, medicine bottles, and milk. "He's probably in the drawing room," Beatrice said over her shoulder as we moved through the dining room and across the entry hall. She pushed open the drawing room door. "It's me, Edwin. I've brought you some fish and chips and a visitor."

Mr. Wallings, situated in his chair with a tray of food in front of him, greeted Beatrice and shoved the bowls around to make room for the Styrofoam container that Beatrice handed him. "Hello, Miss Sharp—or is it Ms.? Or even Mrs. Sharp?" he asked. "So confusing these days."

Impressed that he even remembered my name at all, I said, "Kate. Call me Kate." His physical movements might be slow, but mentally he was quick.

"All right, Kate. We will be seeing a lot of you around here, I hope." He paused as he opened the box and inhaled deeply.

"Smells divine, Beatrice. Thank you. Look at the mush they feed me. Can't get my strength back on gruel."

"But you do have one of Sherry's custards there," Beatrice pointed out as she placed her sunglasses on a side table. "They are amazing," she said to me as she settled into a wingback chair near Mr. Wallings. I avoided the saggy couch, instead perching on a tufted footstool.

Beatrice said, "Might I have a taste of the custard? Doesn't look as if you're going to eat it."

"I'm sure Eve will get you some," Mr. Wallings said, but Beatrice picked up the bowl.

"No need. A bite or two is all I want."

Mr. Wallings looked at me. "Did you bring the paperwork along this time?"

"No, I didn't. I'm sorry. I haven't had time to get it together."

Beatrice said, "I kidnapped her from the pub. She's going to take some photos of the drawing room now that the scaffolding is down." She ate a bite. "Sherry must have changed her recipe. There's a hint of something else. Can't place it."

Footsteps sounded from the entry hall, and I swiveled toward the door, bracing myself for Eve's displeasure. She wasn't happy to see me, I could tell that right away, but her uncle must have made it clear that he would have his way with the filming because she nodded to me politely, if a little stiffly, then turned to Beatrice. "Beatrice, don't eat that. Let me get you your own serving. That has been sitting out."

Beatrice waved her spoon. "Don't trouble yourself. It's fine."

"No, I insist." She hurried across the room and took the bowl, which Beatrice surrendered. "And you've brought Uncle Edwin lunch. How nice of you," she said in a tone that indicated the complete opposite of her words.

"Don't be such a stickler, Eve. A little pub food won't hurt him."

"Just what I need," Mr. Wallings declared.

"I'll just get you that custard," Eve said to Beatrice. "Would you like some tea?"

"Don't bother on my account," Beatrice said. "And don't bring any more custard. I shouldn't have eaten what I did. In fact, we should be shoving on. I've imposed on Kate and should take her up to the Hall so she can get back to her day."

"It's quite all right," I said, but Beatrice was already standing, her keys in her hand.

She thumped Mr. Wallings' shoulder. "You're looking more like your old self every day. I'm glad to see it."

Mr. Walling said, "It's the company, I'm sure."

"I doubt that. More likely, it's the food. Nothing like Louise's fish and chips to bring you around. Well, we're off. No, don't see us out, Eve. No need. I know the way," Beatrice said briskly, but Eve followed us anyway through the house, carrying the bowl of custard, which she dropped off in the kitchen, then she followed us outside to the car.

Beatrice opened her car door, then patted her pockets. "Left my glasses inside. I'll be right back."

I stepped closer to Eve. "I know you're not pleased with the idea of the production using Coventry House." I'd dealt with reluctant participants before and had found that acknowledging the situation was the best way to go. Directly addressing the issue often diffused some of the tension.

"No, I'm not happy about it. Not in the least. Since I found out about it yesterday, I've done everything I can to convince him to change his mind, and I'll continue to advise him against it."

"But he doesn't seem as if he's interested in changing his mind at all," I said in the mildest tone possible.

"Yes, he can be quite stubborn, but I know what's good for him and what isn't. A movie production with its chaos, the coming and going at all hours, the invasion of privacy—it would be too much. Not to mention the disruption of his schedule, and the possibility of damage to the house."

"We can address all those concerns. Schedules can be worked out so that it's as convenient for you and Mr. Wallings as much as possible, and we will put you up in a hotel. Filming can be restricted to certain areas, and I promise the crew will be extremely careful. I know Alex has worked in grand houses before, and we would only bring in people who would respect and care for the location."

Calling Coventry House a grand house was a bit of a stretch, but I could see Eve liked what I'd said so I continued, "If we continue down this path—if Mr. Wallings doesn't change his mind—I hope you and I can have a good working relationship. We'll be in contact quite a lot since you run Coventry House."

Her posture straightened just a touch, and I knew I'd guessed right—she wanted to be acknowledged as the "lady of the house," the one who ran the show. "That's right. Everything would go to rack and ruin if I wasn't here."

"I'm sure it would."

"In fact, I have to go back. Uncle Edwin always has a bit of a lie down after lunch. I should see to that."

Beatrice emerged from the house, her sunglasses in place. "Will we see you tomorrow, Eve? You are coming to the open house?"

"Of course."

"Wonderful."

Beatrice and I climbed in the car, and I counted it a win that although Eve didn't smile or wave, she did give me a bit of a nod. It wasn't much, but it was a tiny step. The Coventry House thing might work out after all.

"I believe I'll put Eve on the audio returns desk," Beatrice murmured as she navigated through the gates. "Yes, she'd do well there."

"Audio returns?" I asked, noticing that Beatrice was taking the road much slower on the short trip to Parkview Hall.

"We have an audio guide for people who want to listen to a recording as they walk through the house," Beatrice said. "We won't have any of the audio players walking away with Eve on duty. Got the way of a nanny about her. Dependable and efficient, but a bit of a killjoy, if you know what I mean. Edwin did need someone to help him, but I'm afraid she can't see that he's getting better."

"Perhaps she's afraid he won't want her around when he's completely recovered, and she's trying to hold him back as much as possible."

Beatrice frowned. "That may be true. I don't know that she has anywhere else to go. She was made redundant at her job in Manchester. In any case, I don't think Edwin will be able to run the place himself. I should—" Beatrice paused and yawned. "Excuse me. My late night is catching up with me—I should have left the website update until today," she said in aside. "I should mention Eve's future to him. He probably hasn't thought beyond his desire to get rid of the walker."

Beatrice drove over the bridge, then turned down the long drive. We cruised through the forest until Parkview Hall came into view nestled in a fold of rolling green meadow. Beatrice swept the car quickly around to the back of the house, and I wished I had more time to study the design, but I would have time tomorrow at the open house. More time at one of our locations was never a bad thing, and I could indulge my anglophile country home geekishness as much as I wanted. I wouldn't have to be professional and detached, looking for things that could trip up the production.

Beatrice took me through the kitchen and up the back staircase. "The old servant staircase," she explained. "It's faster." We emerged into a wide hallway lined with oil paintings. She pushed open tall, gilded doors, and I reached for my camera. "Beatrice, this room is gorgeous."

Pale gold striped silk lined the walls, rich draperies in the same fabric framed the windows, and a chandelier glittered overhead. Delicate, formal chairs and sofas were spaced around the room, and a harpsichord gleamed in the back corner. Beatrice moved around the room opening the long, narrow interior shutters. "We keep it rather dark, I'm afraid," she said, "Protecting the carpet and fabrics, you know."

I set to work, snapping pictures and writing notes. Beatrice scrubbed her hand over her face and yawned. "I think a strong cup of tea is in order. Would you like some?"

"Sure. I'll close the shutters and find my way down," I murmured, focused on my compass app. I needed to know the orientation of the room, so I could assess the times the sunlight would wax and wane in the room for filming.

Once I had all the photos I needed, I spent a little longer than necessary in the room, just because it was so beautiful. There were a few modern radiators that would have to be concealed, but it wouldn't be that hard to do. I perched on the gold and white striped sofa with curly gilded edges. I could imagine this room as the Netherfield drawing room where Mr. Darcy broodingly watched Elizabeth as Caroline Bingley strove to maintain his attention while she sent barbed comments at Elizabeth.

Time to get back to the real world, I thought as I stood. The sofa creaked ominously, and I froze, fearful for one crazy moment that it would collapse in a heap of dust and splinters, but it didn't. I quickly moved around the room, closing the shutters. I trailed my hand over the burled wood of the harpsichord, then went to find Beatrice.

She was in the kitchen. Her eyes looked a little heavy-lidded, but she rose when I came in and poured me a cup of tea and offered me a plate of what she called "biscuits," but what I would have called crunchy cookies.

Sir Harold arrived and took a seat at the long wooden table with his cup of tea. "You look done in, Beatrice."

"Yes, I know. It's this time of year. Always too much to do and not enough hours leading up to opening day."

"I could come early tomorrow and help, if you'd like," I said.

"Oh, no. I couldn't ask you to do that."

"I'll be here. I plan to come." It wasn't as if I had anything else to do. The investigation into Kevin's death had stalled out it seemed. I'd been checking my phone all day, hoping for a message or a call about the investigation. I supposed Quimby and his team were chasing down all the info they could on Becca, probably confirming exactly when she went to London, and when she returned as well as examining her car's bumper and comparing it to Kevin's rental. I kept all those thoughts to myself. I wasn't sure what I could share or how much of what I knew was general knowledge—probably all of it, I thought, biting into the crumbly biscuit. At the rate news traveled in Nether Woodsmoor, I wouldn't be surprised if Beatrice brought up the news about Becca being at the river with Kevin, but I wasn't going to be the one to broadcast it.

"In that case, come around eight. We can always use an extra set of hands."

I finished my tea, dusted the crumbs from my fingers, and said it was time for me to head back to the inn. Maybe there would be a message for me there. Beatrice offered to drive me, but I said I'd rather walk. "The village isn't far, is it?"

"Only about a mile if you take the footpath that runs along the river." Beatrice peered out the kitchen window then looked to Sir Harold. "But those clouds are thickening again. What do you think, my dear?"

"We might have a few sprinkles, but no real rain until tomorrow morning before sunrise. It will clear out by seven, and we'll have a beautiful day until late afternoon. Best plan on closing around three tomorrow."

"Harold has a knack for predicting rain. He's hardly ever wrong."

I said my goodbyes, put my camera in my tote bag and headed out, taking the path that Sir Harold directed me to at the end of the "car park," as he called it, which cut through a grove of oaks and took me straight down to the bridge. I paused on the bridge and watched the water glide by. The water level had gone down, exposing more of the river bank and the rusticated golden stones of the bridge supports. A few fat raindrops splattered onto the stones beside me and dotted the river.

My phone buzzed with a text. It was from Quimby. *Can you meet me at the inn?*

CHAPTER 16

I HURRIED BACK ALONG THE path to the village as fast as I could. Sir Harold's prediction held true. Except for those few drops at the bridge, the rain held off. Quimby was waiting for me in the inn's entrance hall. Today he had again gone with the monochromatic look, but instead of brown, his color choice for his suit and tie was a light gray.

"Would you mind walking a bit with me, Ms. Sharp? Rather cloudy today, but I'm not able to get out much and enjoy the countryside."

"No, that would be fine." I had my peacoat halfway off, but I shrugged into it again and pushed out through the door.

We crossed the courtyard and moved to the edge of the parking area. "Perhaps the green?" he asked, gesturing toward the path that led to the village.

"Sure." We made the short trek into town silently, passing the church, then the shops and restaurants. The streets were more crowded than I'd seen them. People moved in and out of shops, hurrying along the sidewalk, causing us to weave around them.

"Market Day," Quimby explained. "Farmers bring in fresh

produce, cheese, bread, that sort of thing. They set up in the car park by the Town Hall, if you want to take a look later." The bus stop just short of the green was especially congested with a throng queuing up to board a double-decker bus.

We came to the green and turned in under the arbor that marked the entrance. The wide lawns lined with flowerbeds were deserted except for a couple with a stroller. The area seemed especially quiet and peaceful after the bustle of the street.

Quimby gestured toward one of the park benches. "Not too wet." He swiped his hand along the seat to make sure, and then we sat. I had a million questions in my mind, but made myself be patient. He waited until the couple with a stroller meandered by, then with his gaze on the church tower said, "We received the autopsy report on Mr. Dunn." He swiveled toward me, studying me with his intense green gaze. Somehow, the gray palette of his clothes made his eyes seem more green, at least more intensely green than I remembered.

"It was difficult to pinpoint Mr. Dunn's time of death. The time in the water complicates these things, but they were able to narrow it down to Friday between three and midnight."

"Oh." I'd been tensed, ready for more questions—about the camera memory card or about Becca. I hadn't expected Quimby to give me information from the investigation. I leaned back against the bench and looked out over the swath of grass to a mass of yellow daffodils. "Then that means he was... dead even before I left L.A."

"Yes." Quimby's voice was quiet.

"He was in the water all that time?" My throat felt dry and my vision went a little blurry as I thought of how I'd moved through my weekend, picking up take-out on Saturday, hiking in the San Jacinto Mountains on Sunday afternoon, and heading to Temecula to take pictures on Monday, all without the slightest idea of what had happened to Kevin. It seemed wrong and...almost disrespectful somehow.

"Yes, we think so. Maybe not at the exact location where he was found, but in the water, yes. The report was quite clear on that. There's a significant amount of debris in the water—branches, tree trunks, rocks. His body may have been caught in another location upstream until at some point it broke free and traveled further downstream."

I blinked, and Quimby patted his pockets, then pulled out a small plastic envelope of tissues, which he handed to me.

"Thanks." I wiped my eyes and nose.

"I'm sorry if I've upset you, but I thought you'd want to know. The questions about the time of death seemed to trouble you."

"They did." I crumpled the tissue and reached out to return the packet of unused tissues.

"Keep it. I've got more," he said, making me wonder fleetingly what it would be like to have a job where you routinely carried packets of tissues to hand out to grieving people.

"It's awful to know that it was so long before he was found, but at least now I know that my delay—" I raised my gaze to the clouds. "It sounds so silly now, Marci and me, plotting how to keep everything hidden and quiet. And the whole time, he was already gone." I sniffed and turned back to him. "Were they able to figure out how he died?"

"It's tricky there as well. He had an injury, a blow to the back of the head. It appears he was unconscious when he went in the water. He had some other injuries that we haven't been able to determine the cause of, but they weren't fatal." He paused a moment, then continued, "I've given our liaison officer your contact information. He will help you arrange for the body to be transported back to the States. Normally, we'd work with the family, the next-of-kin, but you are here, and...well," he stopped.

I cleared my throat. "Kevin didn't have much family. In fact, I don't know that he had any relatives at all that he kept in touch with. He used to say we were his family." I felt my throat going prickly, but swallowed and turned to Quimby. His face was so sympathetic that it surprised me, and for a moment I forgot what I was going to say. I cleared my throat. "The... transport of his body will be next week?"

"Yes, I believe so as it's already Friday afternoon."

I nodded and leaned back against the bench, absorbing the quiet peacefulness of the scene in front of me: the stretch of grass, the daffodils bobbing in the slight breeze, and the rise of the solid church steeple, its angular lines standing out sharply against the gray sky. I balled the tissue and stuck it in my pocket along with the packet of unused tissues.

"Do you have any other news about the investigation?" I asked. "That you can share?" I added quickly. This meeting was obviously informational, not interrogatory, and I didn't want him to switch back to asking pointed questions, but I had to see if he'd tell me anything.

"Generally, our liaison officer keeps the family up-to-date on the investigation," he said, and I thought that was his answer, but after a moment he added, "However, this is a special circumstance. You are essentially functioning as next-of-kin, and the time of death information takes you off the suspect list."

"That's good to know. Now that you've marked me off the list, you can focus on some really viable suspects."

The corner of his mouth turned up. "Did anyone ever tell you, you can be quite bossy?"

"Oh, I've been called worse. Much worse. But I prefer single-minded and persistent. I'm sure you're familiar with those qualities?"

He sent me a sideways look as he pulled his phone from his pocket. He flicked through a few screens, then said, "What I can tell you is that we are pursuing several leads in the case. Several good leads."

I waited. He put his phone away.

"That's it?"

"No, of course there's more. I just wanted to see if you'd push for more. Some families don't want the details..."

"I think I've established that I'm interested in the details. I'm a detail person."

"Yes. The Burberry button connection proves that. As far as that goes, Becca Ford's vehicle is under examination, and we've confirmed that she did go to London after she met with Mr. Dunn at the river. We haven't been able to eliminate her as a suspect."

I narrowed my eyes. "Is that police-speak, meaning that you think she did it but can't prove it?"

"As I told you earlier, I suspect everyone. And that is all I can tell you about Mrs. Ford."

"What about Frank Revel?" I asked.

"He was on his way to the airport when he met with Mr. Dunn. We have confirmed that after their argument, he drove to the airport in Manchester and left on a business trip. Conference in Ireland. He returned Monday afternoon."

"So he's off the list," I said. Quimby didn't reply. "Is there anyone else on this list of yours besides Becca?"

"That information, I can't share with you."

"What about Kevin's camera? Were there any fingerprints on it?"

Quimby shook his head. "You don't forget much, do you?"

"Part of my job. Scouting and managing locations requires lots of detail work."

"Hmm. No, no fingerprints."

"None?"

"No. Interesting, that."

"I'd also wondered why you asked me if I smoked?"

"Oh, that. We found cigarette butts at the clearing where Mr. Dunn's car went in the water. We have to check everything. They were unrelated to the case and had probably been there for weeks." Before I could ask another question, Quimby changed the subject. "Now, about the inquest, you received word that it will be next week?"

"Yes, Tuesday. And I'll have to answer questions?"

"That's right. It's nothing to worry about. It's not a trial like you're familiar with in the States. The inquest determines the cause of death. You'll only be asked about the discovery of the car and possibly about Mr. Dunn's business since you were an employee." He stood. "As I said, it's nothing to worry about."

I stood as well. "Easy, peasy. Right. I'll try to remember that."

"Exactly." He flashed a smile at me that transformed his face, making him look almost handsome. "Can I walk you back to the inn?"

"Thanks, but I'd like to see the church. I haven't been inside."

"Then I'll see you next week."

I nodded. "Thank you for telling me about Kevin." It had been kind of him to personally give me the news rather than telling me over the phone. "I appreciate it."

He nodded and left. I made my way around the green, walking beside the nodding daffodils until I reached the church. I climbed the shallow steps, which were slightly grooved toward the center—from so many feet treading in and out of the church for hundreds of years, I supposed. The heavy studded wooden door was unlocked. I opened it a few inches, slipped inside, and took a seat in one of the back pews. Sturdy columns marched down each side of the church, supporting gothic arches. The pointed arches were echoed everywhere in the design, from the interior doorways to the mullioned windows. I gazed around the interior with its coved recesses and intricate detailing. I loved the way the pale light filtered through the ornate windows. I wanted to get some pictures—I had my camera in my tote bag, but I didn't know if photography was allowed, and it might seem disrespectful, so I left it where it was.

I don't know how long I sat there, thinking about Kevin and how good he'd been to me. My family had been occasional churchgoers when I was little, but then we'd tapered off to only attend on the major holidays. I sent up a prayer for Kevin and any of his long-lost family that might be out there, then stood to leave.

A figure on the other side of the aisle mirrored my actions and moved toward me, meeting me at the back of the church near the door where I'd entered.

"Hey," Alex said in a hushed tone. "I saw you come in, but I didn't want to disturb you."

"I wanted to see inside. It's beautiful and very grand."

"Bit surprising to find such an edifice in tiny little Nether Woodsmoor, yes."

We moved through the door and paused on the steps outside. Alex said, "I was passing through town. I have some work to get back to, but wanted to make sure you knew about the open house at Parkview Hall tomorrow. Have you heard about it?" There was something in his manner, a hesitancy, that wasn't like his usual easy-going personality.

"Yes. Beatrice invited me. I'm going early in the morning to help her."

"Oh. Excellent." He was suddenly busy with the scarf at his neck, retucking it into the collar of his leather jacket. "Well. I won't be there until late morning. Another appointment. Perhaps I will see you there." He moved down the steps before I could answer.

I stood there with the distinct feeling that he'd intended to ask me out on a date, and I'd managed to give the impression that I would have turned him down, all without being quick enough to realize what he was about.

I followed him down the steps more slowly. His pace was quicker than mine, and the next time I spotted him, he was across the street. Not that I wanted to catch up with him or anything. It would just be nice to make sure there wasn't a misunderstanding. We were working together. It was important to stay on good terms. But he was too far away. I'd have to look for him tomorrow.

I moved down the street and passed the bus stop where two buses waited and a mass of people milled around on the sidewalk. I shuffled and edged my way through the crowd. At the crosswalk, as I reached to push the button to activate the light, something pressed against my ankle. At the same moment, a solid shove between my shoulder blades propelled me off the sidewalk.

I fell into the street, landing hard on the one hand that I managed to get out to break my fall. Pain shot up through my arm to my shoulder, and my focus narrowed to the gritty asphalt of the street, which was only an inch from my face. Far away, it seemed, I heard a commotion of raised voices, the skidding sound of brakes on wet pavement, then voices and words flowing around me.

People closed around me. Legs and shoes came into view, blocking out the car bumper a few feet from the crosswalk as I rolled onto my knees and pressed my palms onto the mud and damp of the street to push myself up.

"Are you all right, luv?"

"These Americans, they never look the right way, do they?"

"So impatient. Couldn't even wait for the light."

"I'm okay."

One strong hand fastened under my uninjured arm, all but levitating me to a standing position. I looked up into Quimby's green eyes and his worried face. "Are you injured?" he asked.

"No, I think...I'm okay." I moved my right arm, stretching it and flexing my hand experimentally. All my fingers worked, but I had an ugly red graze on my palm.

"Here you are, luv," said the woman who'd been the first one to check on me. She handed me my tote bag. "I gathered up your things. They are all in there. A bit dirty, but nothing broken or lost, I think."

"Oh, thank you." I spotted my camera still snuggled into the bottom corner of the bag. At least it hadn't been broken.

The woman ran an assessing glance over Quimby and seemed to decide he had everything in hand. She patted my shoulder. I tried to hide my wince. "Next time wait for the signal and look to the *right*. So important, not to forget. To your right." She departed, and the rest of the people who'd been lingering dispersed.

"Do you need to sit down?"

"No. I'm okay, but I didn't forget to look. I wasn't trying to cross the street at all. I was reaching for the crosswalk button when something tangled in my feet, and then someone pushed me."

CHAPTER 17

QUIMBY ESCORTED ME BACK TO the inn, careful to avoid touching my right arm and shoulder. At the inn, a woman with wispy brown hair and delicate features at the front desk turned out to be Tara, who efficiently cleaned and bandaged my hand, then brought Quimby and me plates of scones and a pot of tea. For some reason, I expected Quimby to turn down the food, but he inhaled it, drank his tea, and waited until I'd eaten as well before he said, "Did you see anyone you recognized around you before you were pushed?"

"So you believe me?"

"Yes. I don't think you're the type of person to exaggerate, and you were very definite that you felt a push on your back."

"A shove, yes. Between my shoulder blades."

"It is hard to mistake a shove for an accidental brush against someone. So did you see anyone you recognized?"

"No, I wasn't paying attention. I moved through the group around the bus stop, but I didn't see any familiar faces there. At the crosswalk, I was only looking at the button to set off the light. I didn't look around to see who was near me."

"And what did you do between the time we talked and you approached the crosswalk?"

"I went to the church. Alex was there. We spoke for a few minutes, then he left."

"Alex Norcutt?"

"Yes, but he was already gone by the time I got to the crosswalk. I saw him on the other side of the street. He was there before I even reached the bus stop."

"He could have doubled back."

"But he doesn't have a reason to hurt me." I didn't mention the possible quasi-date turn down. I wasn't even sure if he'd meant to ask me out. And people didn't normally go around shoving people in the street, even if they'd been turned down. Quimby took his time pouring himself another cup of tea. He raised his eyebrows in a question and gestured with the teapot to my cup. I shook my head. He put down the teapot, added sugar to his tea, and stirred. "You asked me quite a few questions earlier, but you didn't ask about Alex Norcutt. You aren't curious about him?"

"Curious?"

"About his alibi."

"No, I just thought that…" I trailed off remembering the conversation Alex and I had coming down from Strange Hill when I'd asked him, almost flippantly, if he'd hurt Kevin. He'd said no. I'd believed him.

"You trust him. The two of you may not be in a relationship, but I can see there is a rapport between you."

"I didn't lie to you earlier. I'd never met Alex before I arrived here."

"Yes. I know. I'm not accusing you of lying. I'm simply pointing out that there is an affinity. It's obvious. Just remember that you don't know him."

"Are you saying I shouldn't trust him?"

"He has no alibi from Friday afternoon until Saturday night.

He says he was home alone Friday, then drove to Manchester and back on Saturday, looking for new locations."

"That's routine in our line of work."

"But he has no photographs to show for it. Says his camera malfunctioned, and he has sent it off for repairs. He says he's currently using a spare camera."

"Oh."

"Yes. So just be wary."

I didn't want to be wary of Alex. "But surely it could have been someone else? What about Becca? She can't be too fond of me."

"A woman like Becca would be hard to miss, even in a crowd."

"She could have been disguised, I suppose," I said. "I know that's reaching, but I don't think Alex would...he just seems too kind to have done anything like that."

Quimby looked at me with a trace of pity in his gaze.

"Doesn't England have cameras everywhere, recording everything? Can't you check those?"

"Nether Woodsmoor is not London or Manchester. I will check, but I don't think the camera network here is quite as extensive."

"And what would be the point of pushing me? Whether it's Becca...or Alex, as much as I don't like to even think it of him, why would either one...or anyone, push me?"

"I don't know. And that's what worries me," Quimby said with a sigh. "Perhaps you know something that you don't realize you know. Perhaps you've seen something, photographed something, that could be dangerous to the killer. You must be cautious."

Quimby had me recap the last few days, all my activities, who I had talked to, where I had gone, as he made notes on his phone. When we finished, he put his phone away and said, "If it weren't for the inquest, I might have you leave, but with it coming up so quickly, you'd better stay. Please be careful. Very careful."

DRAINED AND ACHY, I trooped up to my room, took some Advil and looked at every photo I'd taken since I'd arrived in Nether Woodsmoor, but didn't find anything that looked remotely suspicious or incriminating. I tried reading my Agatha Christie book, but I couldn't concentrate and put it down. I dropped into bed, wondering if I should go to the open house at Parkview Hall the next morning. Would it be safer to stay in my room?

I slept fitfully, my mind busily running over the events of the last few days. At six-thirty, after shifting from side to side and listening to raindrops tap against the window for over an hour, I threw the covers back and went to shower. I'd go to the open house. Sitting around my room might be "safe," but there was a high probability that it would drive me crazy. Besides, I'd be surrounded by people at the open house. I pushed away the thought that I'd been surrounded by people immediately before I was pushed in front of a car. There were no busy roads at Parkview Hall. I'd stay clear of anyone on Quimby's suspect list (i.e. Becca) and everything would be fine. I'd even give Alex a wide berth.

Dressed in layers—a long-sleeved chambray shirt over a tank-top and jeans, a floral scarf, and my trusty calf-high boots —and holding a cup of coffee, I made my way to my rental car. I wasn't sure if I'd be working inside or outside, but I figured I had it covered with the layers and the boots. I didn't even have to unfurl the umbrella tucked under my arm. Sir Harold had been right; the rain had stopped, and a stiff breeze was sweeping the clouds from the sky. My hand and arm were still sore, but another dose of Advil helped take the edge off the pain. I was thankful the car was an automatic and that I didn't have to use my sore hand to change gears.

I backed out of the inn's parking lot and navigated the short drive to Parkview Hall, managing to stay on the left side of the road. The traffic was thin, and I didn't have any trouble, and I only fleetingly wondered if Alex would have picked me up in his MG if I hadn't said I was going in the morning. I didn't see his little red car anywhere in the throng of vehicles already parked in the paved lot at Parkview Hall. In my frantic run up the drive on the day we'd found Kevin's car, I'd completely overlooked the turnoff to the parking area tucked neatly behind the trees. It was where Sir Harold had directed me yesterday when I took the path back to the village.

The lot was already half full, and I followed a sign that proclaimed the "Manor House" was to be found at the end of a narrow trail. I followed a group of three women along the trail, which wound through the grove of stately trees. I paused as I emerged from the trees to take in the front of Parkview Hall. I'd been too flustered the first time I'd seen it when Beatrice and I were hurrying through the woods to really look at the building of honey-colored sandstone.

A divided staircase curved up to the central block of the house, leading to the portico with six imposing Corinthian columns. Wings extended out on each side, and rows of windows topped with triangular pediments marched along the two upper stories of the house above the rusticated ground floor. Glowing in the rising sun, the stone seemed even more buttery and golden than it had the first day I'd seen it.

I drank in the elegant lines, then followed the signs to the entrance at the side of the house, not the grand doors at the front. Here, more people mingled and chatted as they clipped on nametags.

"Kate!" a voice called, and I turned to see Beatrice making her way toward me. "So good of you to come. I see you already have coffee, but if you'd like anything to eat, help yourself." She pointed to a table set up to the side with breakfast breads and fruit.

"I ate at the inn."

"Then let me show you around. Entrance to the house here, up those steps. Formal gardens that way." She pointed across a wide grassy area enclosed with shrubbery to an arched gateway. "Along with the maze and the folly. There's an exit from the house to the gardens as well. On the other side of the house, we have the children's play area, which is next to the old stables and carriage house. Today everything is open, but on regular days people can purchase a ticket to tour the house, or a ticket for the gardens, or a combo ticket. I thought perhaps you'd like to be inside the house today? I need someone to count visitors and hand out maps."

"I can do that."

"Brilliant."

I followed Beatrice indoors. She moved quickly through a small room set up with a counter and cash register to a black and white checkerboard tiled entrance hall with a lofty ceiling, a huge fireplace, and a wide marble staircase covered in an ornate red runner patterned with blue, green, and yellow. The staircase rose to a second floor gallery that wrapped around the entire entry hall. Overhead, a scene from Greek mythology played out on the ceiling.

Beatrice took me to a Sheraton table in one corner of the hall, scrawled my name on an adhesive nametag with a marker, gave me a metal clicker so I could count each visitor who entered the hall, and pointed out a stack of maps to hand out. "Mona is on duty in the hall this morning." She nodded to a narrow-faced woman in a navy blazer hovering at the foot of the stairs. "She'll chat with visitors, answer any questions they have about the history of the building or the furnishings, and generally keep an eye on things."

A frazzled bald man scurried over to Beatrice. No one could find the keys to unlock the restrooms in the garden area. I told Beatrice that I would be fine, and she strode off to handle the emergency.

The morning passed quickly. At nine, a trickle of visitors, some with audio guides draped around their necks, flowed into the hall. I clicked off the correct number on the ticker and handed out maps. Mona hovered, providing tidbits of info on how the hall had been part of the original house and dated from the fourteenth century, and how it had been modernized by a renovating baronet in the late 18th century.

A little after ten, another woman in a navy blazer shepherded a group of people on a guided tour into the hall. There was a lull in visitors, and her voice carried, so I was able to listen to her as she described the history of the hall in more detail as well as a little background on how the house was run. "Early each morning housemaids would remove the ashes from the fireplace, dust the furniture, and sweep the floor. Their duties were to be completed out of sight of the family and houseguests. They had separate staircases and passageways so that they could move through the house unseen. We'll take one of those passageways later from the kitchen to the upstairs bedrooms, a trek that the servants would have made many times each day, often carrying buckets and jugs of heated water for the ladies and gentlemen of the house to bathe in..." Her voice faded as she moved away, guiding her group to the next room, and I thought about the peculiarity of the worlds of the gentry and the servants coexisting in such close proximity yet separated so completely.

Another large group entered the hall, and I didn't have time to think about class distinctions. The flow of visitors increased steadily as it drew closer to noon. A little after twelve, a woman of about twenty with a smattering of freckles and frizzy red hair spilling over her navy blazer popped up by my side, and told me she was there to relieve me for the afternoon shift. "Beatrice said to tell you thank you so much. She's tied up giving a tour of the gardens at the moment, or she'd be here herself." She handed me an audio guide. "You're welcome to wander through the house and take in the grounds. When you're done, you can turn it in at the audio return desk on the terrace by the tea shop."

I thanked her and turned over the clicker then moved off to the drawing room. I settled the strap of the audio guide around my neck, planning to take in the house, but it was so crowded with visitors that I decided to wait. If things went well and the production continued, I'd be in these rooms more times than I could count. If everything fell through...well, I could return on a less busy day and enjoy them without bumping elbows with strangers. The tour of the house ended, like all good tours, in a gift shop area. I skipped the glossy books and postcards, and pushed through one of the large doors to the terrace.

Café tables dotted the terrace, and a chalk menu board outside a building with a dutch door listed tea, sandwiches, and snacks available. People sat in the sun, eating ice cream and sipping tea. Dogs lay at the feet of a few people, their leashes looped around a nearby chair. A sign over another dutch door at the other end of the building read, "Audio Guide Return."

The grounds were extensive and a lot less crowded than the house, so I set off to find the lake and folly. I'd studied the map enough while I was clicking off visitors that I could find my way. Unlike the grove of trees in the front of the house, the back was wide open, and I wondered if the trees had been cut down or if the open expanse was a natural feature. I moved along a wide sandy path up the gently rising ground until I reached the summit where I stopped to take in the view.

The grounds were even more expansive than I'd imagined. An oval of water glittered in the bright sunlight. On the far side of the water stood a round stone folly with six columns and a domed roof. To the right of the folly was a shrubbery maze, and I could see colorful figures moving through its narrow pathways. The path I was on continued downward to make a loop around the lake, then went on to the maze. I wanted to walk it, but decided I was too hungry to make the trek on an empty stomach. I turned and went back down the path to the teashop. I'd have a quick sandwich and then explore the grounds.

I joined the line to order a sandwich, which was quite long, but it was moving quickly. As I inched forward, I watched a couple with a weary-looking toddler in a stroller approach the matching dutch door at the other end of the building to return their audio guide. A large sign with directions to the car park, the house, and the gardens was propped up on the ledge of the dutch door, blocking my view of the person who took the audio guide. I could only see a pair of feminine hands, long-fingered with clear polish on the nails. I wondered if the person behind the sign was Eve. I was about to shift my gaze back to the panorama of the gardens, but the movement of the hands caught my attention as those long fingers folded the strap of the first audio guide back and forth in an accordion fold, then wrapped the last bit of the strap around the whole thing to hold the folded strap in place against the audio guide. The strap on the second audio guide got the same treatment.

The last time I'd seen a strap accordion folded and held in place like that was when I opened the box containing Kevin's camera.

$\mathcal{T}$HE MAN IN LINE BEHIND me cleared his throat. "Ah, the line has moved."

"Sorry." I shifted to the audio return line behind a voluptuous woman who'd stepped up to the opening. I peered over her shoulder and spotted Eve, who was turned to the side, putting the audio guides into a tray, plugging each one into a charging slot.

The two women obviously knew each other. The curvy woman in front of me didn't have an audio guide to return. She'd just stopped by to chat. I was so fixated on looking at the folded cords that I wasn't really paying attention to what they were talking about, but then Eve dropped her voice, a change that caught my attention. "...should be over by two," she said. "Stay here, in plain sight."

The full-figured woman had been standing casually, but when Eve lowered her voice, she leaned forward over the little ledge that ran across the top of the half door. A dog barked sharply behind me, blocking out their next words.

The barking stopped, and Eve said, "...after that, I'll arrange everything—"

Eve noticed me and abruptly broke off. In a normal tone, she said, "...for your party. Parkview Hall handles many special events. You should speak to Beatrice."

At Eve's change in volume, the other woman stood up straight. "Yes, of course." As she moved away, Eve transferred her gaze to me. "Can I help you, Ms. Sharp?"

"Ah...yes." I fumbled with the audio guide. The strap caught in my hair as I lifted it off my neck. I disentangled it, then handed it over. "I need to turn this in."

"Thank you." Eve took it, efficiently accordion folded the audio guide's cord, and snapped it into place on the charging tray. "Anything else I can help you with?"

I pulled my gaze away from the rows of audio guides, their cords neatly wrapped and stowed with almost military precision. "Ah, no. Thank you," I said, trying for the most normal, casual tone of voice in the world. I must have failed because Eve looked from me to the rows of audio guides. Another cluster of people arrived behind me. I turned and walked through the rows of tables to a path that led away from the terrace.

I moved along the sanded path, not able to take in the sculpted hedges and the flowerbeds. My thoughts were focused on those straps, folded so exactingly. It couldn't be a coincidence that the camera strap had been folded the same way, could it? Probably not.

Had I destroyed evidence by taking the camera out of the box and unfolding the strap? I felt a bit sick and dropped down onto a bench set against a high stone wall out of the way of the main thoroughfare. But then that would mean that Eve had carefully folded the camera strap around Kevin's camera, boxed it up, and somehow dropped it off at the inn without being seen. Why would she do that? Why would she even have the camera in the first place?

I was still in view of the terrace, and there were plenty of people milling about, but I wasn't watching them. I stared at a bed of daffodils, their vibrant yellow contrasting sharply with the dark earth between the plantings, and tried to work out how Eve could have come into possession of the camera. Perhaps she found it? It had Kevin's name on the strap. It was unmistakable. She'd have known it was his.

But then why the secret drop-off at the inn? I'd have thought that if she found it, she would have called Doug and told him she had it. Or she could have dropped it off at the inn with an explanation of how she got it.

But she hadn't done that. The camera had thrown suspicion on me. I sat for a few moments ruminating on that thought.

I'd told Quimby that Kevin usually had his camera on him, but it wasn't found in the car or the river. It had shown up in a box, completely undamaged. The photos on the memory card showed the last place Kevin took photos was Coventry House. He'd left, driven to the bridge where he'd stopped to change a flat. Quimby had said that Kevin's time of death was estimated to be Friday between three and midnight. Since the camera wasn't in his car or on his person, then it seemed the most logical thing to have happened was that Kevin left the camera at Coventry House. Could he have forgotten it there?

It wouldn't be the first time it had happened. There was the time when Kevin, excited about landing a unique house with a retro art deco look, had set his camera down on the owner's coffee table then walked off and left it. We'd had to make the two-hour drive the next day to pick it up. It wasn't a common occurrence for Kevin to leave his camera, but we all forgot things occasionally, and if Kevin had been swept up in the euphoria of landing a perfect—and up to that point off-limits location—he might have accidentally left it behind in his rush to catch his plane.

Questions raced through my mind. If Eve had found it— and the wrapped cord indicated she'd handled it—when had she found it? And why had she dropped it off so stealthily at the inn? To throw suspicion on me? But why would she do that? Surely someone would only do something like that to keep the attention and speculation off themselves or someone they knew and loved.

"Kate, there you are." Beatrice strode along the sand path toward me. She didn't sit down, and I had to put up a hand to block the sun from my eyes as I looked up at her as she spoke. "Thank you so much for your help this morning. Did you get the audio guide?"

"Yes. Thank you."

"Wonderful. Sorry to run, but I must check on the gift shop. Minor catastrophe there. Cashiers can't find the register tape."

"If I could just ask you a quick question…"

"Of course." She'd already taken a few strides away, but returned.

I stood up. "You mentioned that you'd heard last week that Coventry House was going to be used for Longbourn. Is that right, that you heard the news last week?"

"Yes."

"Are you sure?"

Beatrice tilted her head. "Yes. I can even tell you the day. It was last Friday. I remember because I had some books due at the library. I picked up a new spy thriller for Edwin, and dropped it off with him."

"So it was Edwin who told you?"

"Oh no. He didn't mention it. He was in quite good spirits though. I could tell something had happened to cheer him up, but he wouldn't say what it was. He was enjoying keeping his secret to himself. No, it was Eve."

"Eve?"

"Yes, she stopped by that afternoon to drop off some flyers for a ramble she's leading. Wanted them to be here for the open house. We have a display of flyers and brochures of local events in the entrance area."

"And she mentioned that Coventry House was going to be used as a location?" I asked, my thoughts spinning.

"She didn't mention it directly, no. I said how good it would be for Nether Woodsmoor to have the film people in town, and she muttered something about Mr. Dunn getting his hooks into Edwin and using Coventry House for Longbourn."

"She mentioned Kevin specifically?"

"Yes, but I told her I thought it would be good for Edwin."

"And was she upset?"

"Well, yes," Beatrice said reluctantly. "But I told her not to worry too much, that I thought it would work out for the best. I'm glad to see she took my advice. Took her a few days to come around, but she has." Beatrice frowned. "I wish she would have brought Edwin today. She said he's feeling down and gloomy. It would be good for him to get out." Beatrice's gaze strayed from my face to the house. "I'd love to chat longer, but I really must get up to the gift shop."

"Of course." She thanked me again for my help and strode off. I sat back down on the bench with a bump, one thought reverberating in my mind: Eve knew.

She knew last week that Kevin had visited her uncle and obtained permission to use Coventry House. Either from finding the camera or some other way, she'd discovered Kevin's visit to Coventry House, and she hadn't been happy about it. Beatrice didn't see anything untoward in these little facts, but she didn't know what Quimby had told me about Kevin's time of death. He'd died that day. In fact, Eve's route from Parkview Hall to Coventry House would have taken her along the bridge.

I had to call Quimby. I scrolled through my list of recent calls until I found his number. It went directly to voicemail, and I left a rather long, rambling message that probably wasn't extremely coherent. I hung up and considered calling back to leave a more concise message, but decided that would only make things worse. I stood and made my way out of the garden, intending to go to the car and back to the inn. I was heading for the exit without taking in any of the beauty of the place when I heard my name.

I looked around and saw Alex leaning over a stone wall above me, waving. I waved back, and he pointed to a wide set of shallow stairs flanked by urns. I nodded and met him at the top of the stairs. A lean greyhound stood beside him, the dog's leash looped loosely around his hand. He held a white paper bag in his other hand. As I approached, the dog, which had a brindle coat of black and brown, ambled toward me. I reached out and let the dog sniff the back of my hand. "Hello," I said in a low voice. "Who are you?"

"This is Slink. Short for Slinky. I thought I'd bring her along today, let her get a run in." The dog dipped her elegant head under my hand, and I rubbed her ears.

"She's gorgeous." Leggy and lean, the dog looked from Alex to me, her brown-eyed gaze sharp and her ears pinned back against her head. A feeling of relief washed over me as Alex smiled at me. Quimby was wrong. I knew Alex hadn't been involved. It was Eve that I should be wary of, not Alex. "So that *was* you. I saw a little red car from the top of Strange Hill, but there was a dog hanging out the window."

"I bring her along sometimes when I'm scouting." I was relieved that his stilted manner that had been so evident on the church steps was gone.

"I bet you do."

"Yeah, she can smooth over those first awkward minutes so that I can make my pitch."

"Hmm...I'd never thought of adding a dog to my bag of tricks, but I might have to consider it now."

Alex lifted the paper bag. "I was on my way to have lunch at the garden overlook. Want to split a sandwich with me? It's roast beef. There's plenty."

"That sounds great. I am starving." The questions about Eve had driven all thoughts of lunch from my mind, but now that I could smell the scent of toasted bread wafting from the bag, my hunger came rushing back.

With Slink loping along behind us, her long leash dragging on the sand path, Alex led the way through intricately shaped flowerbeds edged with low boxwoods. It was too early in the year for all the flowers to be in full bloom, and most of the beds only had tender green shoots coming up through the dark earth.

He stopped at a bench on the edge of the garden near a balustrade where we could look down over the terrace below and view the sweep of the grounds from the tea shop to the dome of the folly in the distance. Slink settled down and watched us attentively. The light changed, and I looked up. A thick band of dark clouds was rolling in.

Alex removed the sandwich from the bag and handed me half. I peeled back the paper and took a bite. "That's quite a stare she has," I said, looking at Slink.

"Yes, it's her best mooching look. I do feed her, you know. She looks thin, but she's healthy."

"I wouldn't say thin, more like lean." I tilted my head. "She's got that supermodel look—toned and sleek with zero fat. But I don't think she would turn down some of my sandwich."

"She wouldn't. You can save her a bite if you'd like. She'll love you forever, if you do."

"Growing up, I always wanted a dog," I said with a sigh.

"You didn't get one?"

"No. Oh, no. We couldn't have one of those dirty, smelly, messy, and—above all—expensive things." I shifted on the bench, not wanting to dwell on my childhood wishes that hadn't come true. "I thought greyhounds were a bit hyper, but she's very calm." Slink hadn't shifted from her alert pose, her big brown gaze bobbing from Alex to me—or probably from his sandwich to mine, to be more accurate.

"Greyhounds are surprisingly mellow dogs. One good sprint and then they lounge around all day." Alex placed the last bite of his sandwich on the ground. Slink ate it, then looked hopefully to me.

"All right," I said with a laugh. "You've been very good." I broke the last few bites up and fed them to her. She delicately plucked them out of my fingers.

"Softie," Alex said with a shake of his head. He removed two bottles of water from the paper bag and handed one to me. Then he took out a flattened paper cup from the inside of his jacket, flexed it open, and poured some of the water from the second bottle into the cup. He held the cup down for the dog. She dipped her long nose into the cup and drank. When she was finished, she collapsed in a heap, her long legs angled under the bench, tangling with ours, and let out a contented sigh.

Alex took a drink from the water that remained in his bottle and stretched an arm along the back of the bench, his attentive gaze focused on me. "Something has changed. You're different."

"Am I?" I said as lightly as I could. I felt better since I'd made that call to Quimby.

"Yes." Alex tilted his head as he studied me, and I thought of our first meeting, when he'd scanned my room and picked up on the detail of Kevin's suitcases. He was attentive to small things, even my change in mood. I looked out over the gardens, debating whether I should tell him about Eve's lie and the camera, but then I saw the voluptuous woman moving along one of the sandy paths below us.

"Who is that? The curvy-figured woman with the brown hair in the pink sweater and jeans."

"Don't want to talk about it, hmm? Okay." Alex looked in the direction I pointed. "That's Sherry. Cooks for Mr. Wallings." As Alex spoke, a young man approached Sherry. They paused, she said a few words, and touched her watch. The younger man looked at his watch, nodded, then they each walked away in opposite directions.

"That was the gardener from Coventry House," I said slowly. I'd seen him in the garden the day I'd met Mr. Wallings, but I'd seen him somewhere else, too.

Alex dug into the paper bag and removed a chocolate bar. "Not much in the way of pudding—or what you'd call dessert— but it's all I've got." He unwrapped the bar and offered me a square of chocolate, which I ate absently, not really tasting it because I was so absorbed in trying to work out where I'd seen the two people.

"Now, Sherry is an excellent cook," Alex continued. "Makes wonderful custards. Although, she doesn't seem to have a clue about what to use a mortar and pestle for. I was waiting in line behind her this morning to get in and tried to strike up a conversation. There was a very nice granite mortar and pestle in the kitchen in Coventry House, and I asked if she liked it. She looked at me like she had no idea what I was talking about."

I stared at Alex, my thoughts suddenly whirling.

He said, "I have a marble one that I use for pesto and salsa."

Momentarily distracted, I said, "So you're a chef."

"Chef is too pretentious. I know how to cook a few things. Man's got to eat. Anyway, back to Sherry. She's famous for her custards."

"I've heard." I looked back at the panoramic view. Sherry's figure was getting smaller as she moved farther away down the path, but the young man she'd talked to was nearing us. "When Beatrice and I stopped there yesterday, Mr. Wallings didn't want his custard, and Beatrice ate it—" I broke off, remembering where I'd seen Sherry and the gardener before. "By the river," I murmured. "The night I arrived." My thoughts skipped over their conversation. I sat forward on the bench.

Little bits and pieces of odd events and overheard conversations came together. My jumbled thoughts arranged themselves, falling into a pattern that sent my heartbeat thumping. I looked at my watch. It was one-thirty.

I jumped up. "Coventry House. Someone needs to get there quickly."

CHAPTER 19

*A*LEX, WHO HAD BEEN LOUNGING back against the bench, sat forward. Slink popped her head up and watched us from her prone position. "What's wrong?" Alex asked.

"I can't explain. It would take too long. I have to find Beatrice. Sorry. Thanks for lunch," I called as I sprinted away, zigzagging through the people strolling in the garden. As I hit the stairs that flowed down the terrace, I pulled out my phone. I kept moving as quickly as I could while I found Quimby's number. The call went straight to voicemail again.

I blew out a sigh of exasperation as I waited for the beep. "This is Kate Sharp. Look, I know this is going to sound crazy, but you need to get to Coventry House right away. It's urgent— an emergency. It's one-thirty now. You need to get there as fast as you can. It has to be before two." I was sucking in a breath to continue the message when a beep cut me off. I pocketed my phone. No help there.

I hurried over to the tea shop, scanned faces, looking for Beatrice, but I didn't see her anywhere. Eve was still at her post.

A man in a navy jacket moved by me. I caught his sleeve. "Beatrice Stone. Where is she?"

"She's taken the next tour up to the folly, I believe."

By the time I got up there and explained everything, it would be too late. I headed for the exit gate. As I pushed through, a streak of black and brown fur zipped by me, a long leash trailing out behind it. Alex caught up to me, his arm extended to give Slink as much leash as possible. He whistled, and the dog notched down her speed, shortening her long stride, and galloped back to us.

"What's the hurry?" Alex asked.

"I have to get to Coventry House. I called Quimby but he's not answering—" I stopped short. My car, parked in what had been a neat row first thing this morning, was now blocked in by several cars angled into spots that weren't really parking slots. "I'll never get out of there. Where's your car?"

"I'm afraid I can't give you a lift. I walked."

I let out a groan and looked at my watch. One-forty now.

"But if you want to get to Coventry House," Alex said, "there is a footpath on the other side of the bridge. It would probably only take a few minutes. There's a short cut from here to the bridge, too."

"Show me."

Alex set off briskly, making for the path I'd taken yesterday, Slink trotting at his side. The path curved and dipped through a copse thick with undergrowth. It wasn't long before I heard the whisper of running water, and we were on the road. We crossed the bridge, and Alex pointed to another footpath that branched off the road. "This path goes to Coventry House."

"Thanks," I said and hurried by him, almost at a sprint.

Slink jogged along beside me for a moment, then stretched out her long legs, easily pulling away from me. Alex trotted up beside me. "So you want to tell me what's going on?"

The path narrowed, and tall trees closed in on each side.

The heavy dark clouds had moved directly overhead, blotting out any trace of blue sky, making the forest even darker and gloomier. Alex dropped back slightly, but Slink stayed in the lead.

"I don't think I could explain it—it's too convoluted—and I don't know that you'd believe me. I don't have any proof, just a suspicion. But if I'm right—" I broke off, not wanting to think about what could happen if I was right.

"Try me."

"Okay," I drew a deep breath then said, "It is several things —bits and pieces, really—that don't seem that significant, but when I put them together, they make a frightening patchwork-quilt-kind of sense. Like Celia. Do you know her?"

"Yes, she worked at Coventry House."

"Until Eve let her go." I swiped a low tree branch aside as we half-walked, half jogged along the narrow, twisting trail. "Nothing odd in that, right? Except that Beatrice says Celia is an excellent, conscientious employee, while Sherry, the person Eve hired is, well, apparently a slacker."

"Doug and Tara didn't seem heartbroken to see her leave the inn," Alex said.

"So why fire a good employee and hire a worse one?"

"Maybe Celia and Eve didn't get along."

"I think it was more than that," I said. "I think that Eve knew Celia wouldn't go along with her plans for Mr. Wallings."

"What plans?"

"To have him change his will to favor her before she killed him."

I turned because Alex had stopped dead. "You do realize what you're saying?" he asked.

"Yes, I do. That's why I'm so freaked out. Firing Celia cut off Mr. Wallings from a long-time employee. It isolated him. Eve comes in, takes over everything, the running of the house, the care of Mr. Wallings."

I could see the unbelief on his face, so I hurried on. "The mortar and pestle—there's a reason Sherry has no clue what to use it for. She's not using it for cooking. She's using it to grind up pills to put in Mr. Wallings' food, probably sleeping pills in his custard, judging by Eve's reaction when she saw Beatrice eating Mr. Wallings' serving the other day. Didn't you notice the pill bottles when we walked through the house?"

"No."

"Well, I did. Things like that catch my attention, I guess. I had to move in with my mom for a while after the divorce. I had to keep an eye on all her medicine. I recognized some of the names on the pill bottles when I moved Mr. Wallings food tray the other day. When I went back with Beatrice, those pill bottles were in the kitchen on the island with the food ingredients."

"You've been back to Coventry House? With Beatrice?"

"Oh, I can't stand here and explain, it will take too long to make you understand." I turned and trotted away, moving as fast as I could over the rough, snaking trail.

Alex was at my shoulder in a moment. "In his custard, you said?"

"Yes," I talked as we moved. "He gave it to Beatrice and Eve nearly ripped it out of her hands when she saw it, insisting it wasn't fresh and that she should get another serving for Beatrice, then later that afternoon Beatrice could hardly keep her eyes open. She said she'd been up late the night before, but now that I think about it, the drowsiness hit her very quickly."

"So you think Eve and Sherry are drugging Mr. Wallings? But why? To make him easier to deal with?"

"It may have started out like that, but no, I think the real reason is so that he will be groggy and won't realize what paperwork he's signing. He told Eve he didn't want to do any bills or paperwork or signing things that day in the garden. Apparently, she brings those things to him in the afternoon before he naps. If he's sleepy and mentally fuzzy, how hard would it be to slip in an extra check made out to her, or a power of attorney, or even a new will?"

We came to a dry stone wall. Slink leapt lightly over it. Alex gripped my hand and steadied me as I climbed over. "And you think that's already happened, that he's signed a new will?"

"I'm afraid it may have. Remember the paperwork that fell off the table? When Mr. Wallings looked through it, he said it should be in his desk. There was a will there. I saw it. And, on the night I arrived in Nether Woodsmoor, I was visiting the pubs, looking for Kevin, and I stopped to look at the river. Two people, a young man and an older woman, walked by. It was Sherry and the gardener from Coventry House. I heard a bit of their conversation. He was worried, feeling guilty I think, about 'witnessing' something. The woman cut him off before he could say anything else and said that they'd only signed a paper."

"A new will would require witnesses," Alex said grimly.

"Something that Celia probably wouldn't have done for Eve."

"So you think the will has been signed for several days?"

"Yes. I don't know what Eve's plans were. Maybe she was going to file it away and wait before doing anything, but then Kevin interfered with her tightly run world at Coventry House. After speaking with him, Mr. Wallings seemed intent on taking back the reigns of the household, so to speak. Kevin forced her hand. There's Coventry House," I said. The trees had thinned, giving away to a wide green field. I could see the boundary hedge that enclosed the gardens of Coventry House.

Alex pulled out his cell phone, dialing as he walked. He tilted the phone away from his face and spoke to me as he listened to it ring. "But why today?"

"They all—Eve, Sherry, and the gardener—all have an alibi. I heard Eve tell Sherry to make sure she stayed at the open house until after two. 'It will be over by then' is what she said. I didn't realize what it could mean or make the connection until you told me that it was Sherry speaking to the gardener. That was when everything matched up and made sense in an awful way."

Alex closed his eyes briefly, then snapped them open as he spoke into the phone, requesting an ambulance at Coventry House.

"What do you think she's done?" Alex asked.

"I don't know. I suppose the easiest thing would be to put an overdose of sleeping pills in his food. Then she could go home, clean up the food, and arrange everything so that it looked as if he decided to do it himself. She did mention to Beatrice that he was feeling down and gloomy today, but that may be a cover for later. We only have her word that he's depressed. She could be lying."

We arrived at the hedge that enclosed Coventry House's garden and followed it around to the gate under the arch of shrubbery. The gate wasn't locked, and we sprinted across the lawn with Slink galloping ahead of us, her long legs splaying then flexing, barely seeming to touch the grass. Alex reached the back door to the kitchen first and stepped back after twisting the doorknob. "Locked."

"The terrace?" I asked, already moving in that direction. "Maybe one of the French doors..."

Alex nodded and whistled for Slink, who had paused, sides heaving as Alex tried the door. We dodged through the garden. As we trotted up the shallow steps to the terrace, relief washed over me. Two of the long French doors stood open. I stepped over the threshold and glanced around the empty drawing room. A tray of food, the plates and bowls smeared with crumbs and streaks of food, sat on a table near Mr. Wallings' camelback chair.

"Bedrooms," Alex said, and I nodded.

"Eve said he naps every day after lunch." We moved through the hall, our feet and Slink's claws clattering across the floor. I took the stairs two at a time, Slink easily loping up the steps between us. At the top, Alex turned left. "Since he didn't show us these bedrooms during his tour, this is probably where his and Eve's rooms are." We barely checked our pace at the first door, which was open, because we could see the room was empty.

The next door was wide open. We could both see a figure lying completely still on the four-poster bed. Some of the interior shutters had been closed, blocking off the daylight, but pale light filtered into the room from a few partially open shutters on the other side of the room.

Breathing hard from all the running and the sprint up the stairs, I took a few steps into the room. The figure in the bed was Mr. Wallings. I could tell by the patch of snowy white hair on the pillow. He was turned away from me, toward the dark side of the room. I took a few steps around the end of the bed until his face came into view. I sucked in my breath. "He's pale —so pale, and his lips are blue," I whispered. Even in the dim room, his skin looked wrong. "We're too late." I turned back to Alex, then started.

Eve stood behind Alex with an antique shotgun tucked into her shoulder, her face stormy. Alex saw the change in my expression and spun around.

"No, don't move," Eve said, as the end of the gun quivered back and forth between us. A foot or two of space separated us. I was around the edge of the bed while Alex had stopped at the foot of the bed. Slink, sensing the change in atmosphere, whined and moved around the room.

"Get your dog under control," Eve snapped.

Alex patted his leg, and Slink trotted in a circle around Eve, her long leash trailing along the ground behind her. Alex put his hand on Slink's back as she settled next to his leg. Her whine softened. Eve motioned with the gun, and both Alex and I tensed. "Closer. Get closer," she commanded.

I inched forward, afraid to make any sudden movements. Alex must have felt the same way because he took a slow step to the side, which brought us within inches of each other. Alex had his hand on Slink's collar, and she shadowed his movements.

"Good. At least you can follow directions." Eve's face was flushed, and there was a brightness in her eyes that I hadn't seen before.

"Ms. Wallings—" Alex began, his tone soothing.

"Shut up. You are a troublemaker. Always have been, right from the start. Interfering and mucking up everything." She was visibly trembling—with rage, I realized. The barrel of the gun bobbed and twitched. Her gaze fastened on me. "And you Hollywood people, especially that Kevin Dunn, making it worse with his plans and ideas, stirring up Uncle Edwin. I knew it when I saw you running out the exit at Parkview Hall today. I heard you asking for Beatrice, and I remembered you hovering behind Sherry, eavesdropping. I knew you'd over-heard enough to work out what had happened. I could see it on your face." She drew in a deep breath and blew it out. The barrel steadied. "But I can still fix it, as I always do. The discovery of my dear uncle's death will have to be delayed until you are…removed."

"You can't seriously think that you can, well…get rid of us?" Alex said in a calm tone. "Without anyone finding out? That's unbelievable."

"I'm a resourceful person, Mr. Norcutt. No one seems to understand that—or how hard I work. Do you know how diffi-cult it is to run a house of this size single-handedly, seeing to the constant repairs, not to mention maintaining the grounds and gardens as well as dealing with a querulous old man? Is there any gratitude? Any appreciation? No. Not one word of thanks. And after giving up my life, my friends to care for him. His own children wouldn't do that for him. I'm the one who dropped everything to be here with him. One would think the least he could do would be to say a word of thanks every once in a while."

"But that doesn't justify killing him," I said.

She continued as if I hadn't spoken, "He wasn't even going to pay me for all my hard work, not anything significant. I asked him, one day right before he drifted off for his nap. I asked him what he planned to do for me. If he intended to make a provision for me. After all, I've done more than his children. It's only right that he include me in his will. The amount he named was a pittance." She raised her chin. "So, I took steps to ensure I get what I'm due. It's only fair."

"It's all about the money?" I asked.

"Of course it's about money," Eve said derisively. "Everything comes down to money in the end, doesn't it? So easy to say money isn't important, but you'll notice the people saying money doesn't matter always seem to have plenty of it. And I deserve to have plenty of it myself." Her hands gripping the gun tightened. "You two are only a little glitch, which can be corrected. Apparently, it's extremely difficult to find a buried body. There was a tremendously informative special on the telly about a serial killer. Did you know, he buried six bodies, *six*, and they weren't discovered until he led the police to them."

"We've called for an ambulance," Alex said in the same calm tone he'd used earlier. I blinked and looked away from her pink cheeks and glittery eyes, feeling a bit like a cobra that had just broken free of the snake charmer's gaze. I'd never seen anyone so convinced, so sure of herself. It was fascinating in a bizarre way.

"I will send it away. I'll explain the call was a mistake, a misunderstanding."

"But that will look odd," I said, "Later, when you call to report that your uncle has died. The fact that you turned away an ambulance shortly before he died will raise questions. It would be better to let them in, talk to them now. You can explain everything. I'm sure they'll understand." I tried to put as much persuasion into my tone as possible, but even to me, my words sounded unconvincing.

As I spoke, I glanced around the room for something that we could use to incapacitate her, but we were isolated in the center of the room with nothing at hand. My pockets were empty, except my cell phone, and short of throwing it at her, I didn't see how I could use it as a weapon. And even if I did throw it at her, she'd probably dodge it, then fire the gun.

"I doubt that," Eve said. I snuck a glance out of the corner of my eye at Alex. If we could charge her...the distance wasn't too large, only a few feet, but we'd have to move together, and there was the chance that she'd get a shot off before we could knock the barrel out of the way. I thought of what a shot at such close range could do to a person, and discarded that idea. I leaned forward a centimeter to look at Slink, but she was standing obediently at Alex's side. She didn't look like the type of dog that would have been trained to charge and attack. My mind scrolled through those thoughts in seconds, considering, then discarding options, feeling more and more desperate as I went down the list.

Then I noticed Slink's leash, which had trailed along on the floor as she milled about nervously before Alex called her to his side. One portion of the leash had fallen so that it curved around, making a complete circle. Eve's right foot was planted in the dead center of it.

The loop that made the handle of the leash was near my foot. I shifted my weight and inched my foot toward the loop.

Alex had noticed my movement, and shot me a quick glance while Eve looked at her watch. I raised my eyebrows and stared at the loop of the leash positioned around Eve's foot.

"Such a shame for you that the nearest ambulance is in Upper Benning," Eve said. "Takes quite a while to get here. In fact, my assistants may arrive before it does. I'll have two people to help me, one of them a strong young man."

Out of the corner of my eye, I saw Alex run his right hand along Slink's collar and unhook the leash. He flexed his hand, looping the leash so that it ran around the back of his hand and into his palm, giving him a tight grip on it. "How do you know they'll help you?" I asked, trying to hold her gaze so she wouldn't look down. "Your young man felt guilty witnessing a will. He might balk at moving bodies." I shifted my foot as imperceptibly as I could, working my toe into the loop of the handle.

"Money, Ms. Sharp," Eve said. "It is quite a motivator."

We were close enough that I could touch the back of Alex's hand with mine. He caught my hand in his and squeezed it once, firmly, then again. He was counting down for us, I realized and for a crazy moment, I wondered if we were going on *three* or a beat after *three*. But then a second before he squeezed my hand again a rustling sound came from behind me, and Eve gave a startled gasp.

"This has gone on long enough, Evie." Even with my back turned, I recognized Mr. Wallings' voice.

Eve shifted the gun so that it pointed between our shoulders.

Alex squeezed my hand, and I jerked my foot backward as hard as I could. The leash bit into the arch of my foot.

Several things happened at almost exactly the same moment. Eve's leg jumped forward, throwing her off balance. She fell in a heap. The bathroom door, which was positioned in the far corner of the darker side of the room and had been closed, banged open, and a police officer ran into the room.

Several other officers flooded into the room from the hall. Quimby was at the front of the pack. He darted forward and plucked the gun out of Eve's hand as the officer who'd come running out of the bathroom restrained her. I was crouching, low to the ground. I didn't remember ducking, but I must have done it instinctively. I decided it was probably the best place for me to be since my legs were suddenly unsteady. I leaned back against the footboard of the bed. Quimby supervised the exit of Eve, who was trembling, too, but she was shaking with outrage, saying how dare the police get involved in a private family matter. She demanded they leave at once.

Quimby handed off the gun to another officer, then stood with his hands on his hips, watching as Eve was escorted down the hall.

I looked at Alex, who stood over me, his hands braced on his knees. Slink stood beside him, her long tail whipping back and forth, her mouth open in a doggie grin, her ears perked up. Despite the chaos going on around her, she sensed the danger was over.

Mr. Wallings moved slowly toward us, his quivery hand braced on the bed. "Are you all right, sir?" Alex asked him.

"I'm fine, just fine, now that I know the truth." His face was a ghostly white and his lips were blue-tinged, but now that he was in the light I could see the changes were due to powder and some sort of colored lip balm. "If you'd be so good as to hand me my cane," he asked, and Alex picked it up from where it had been hooked over the footboard. "I'll wash and rejoin you." He headed for the bathroom at his measured pace.

"Well, that turned out better than I expected it would," I said. Slink came over and licked my chin.

"Yes, would have been nice to know the house was apparently crawling with coppers." Alex sent a dark look at Quimby as he joined us.

"If I'd known you were crashing—literally—our little party,

I would have warned you." Quimby looked around at the police officers moving in and out of the room and then to me on the floor. "Rest here if you need to. Join me in the drawing room when you feel up to it."

I patted Slink's neck. "I think my legs will hold me up now."

Alex and Quimby reached out to help me up. I gave Slink a final pat, then extended a hand to each man and let them hoist me up.

CHAPTER 20

QUIMBY PARTED FROM ALEX AND me on the stairs, saying he'd be with us in a moment. We went into the drawing room and took seats, avoiding the man-eating couch. Slink settled herself on the carpet near Alex's feet with a sigh. Alex had refastened her leash. He draped it over the arm of his chair. Before we had time to speak, Mr. Wallings tottered in, still using his cane. He moved across the room and took a seat in his camelback chair. He removed a handkerchief from his pocket and patted his face and neck. "Feels good to get that powder off my face," he said, and I noticed his collar was damp. "I don't know how you women stand the stuff."

"So you knew about Eve?" I said, feeling like I was the last one to know about a surprise party.

"A few weeks ago, I began to suspect that Evie was skimming money from my accounts. I had to gather proof and get my strength up before I confronted her. Then you handed me that stack of paper with my new 'will,' and I knew the situation was much more serious than I'd realized." He paused, his gaze on the carpet. "I don't understand it. I took her in when she didn't have a job, gave her a place to live. She expected me to give her a portion of my estate—an extremely large portion. But it should go to my children. I didn't expect her to run the place, but," he sighed and shook his head, "she took on more and more, made decisions without consulting me—like getting rid of Celia. There are weeks that are a blur."

"Was she medicating you then?"

"Worked that out, did you? I didn't realize it at that point. Didn't grasp what was going on until I had a little bout with a stomach virus. Couldn't eat a thing for several days, but darned if I didn't feel more clear headed than I had in weeks. From that moment on, I didn't eat a thing she brought me. I've been faking my afternoon lie down as well." He leaned over and opened the lowest drawer in a table beside him, revealing a rainbow of brightly colored energy bars. "These have been in the pantry since my young nephews came to visit last year. Lucky for me they have a shelf life of several decades. I asked Beatrice to bring me a meal occasionally, and I've been fine. I wish I'd been able to stop Beatrice from eating that custard the other day, but I couldn't do that without giving away to Evie that I knew what was going on. I was worried, but Beatrice only ate a few bites, and I knew you were going directly back to Parkview Hall."

I suppressed a shiver. "How fortunate for us that Parkview Hall isn't far. If the drive had been longer..." I paused, not wanting to think about what could have happened.

"If you were going anywhere else, I would have made sure Beatrice didn't drive. I had no idea the effects of the drug on her would be so sudden."

I sat up straight. "Better not to dwell on that, I suppose. What did you do with the food they served you?"

"Said my stomach was still upset. Mostly pushed it around on my plate."

I looked at the tray of plates and bowls with only smears of food on them. "Then, you didn't eat this?"

"Oh, no. That's the fake tray. Quimby's men sealed up the real one and took it off to test it."

"So this was just to fool Eve into thinking that you'd eaten it."

Quimby entered, carrying a tray with tea. He placed it on the table near Mr. Wallings. "The plan was to let Eve wash up the 'incriminating' dishes, which she would believe contained traces of the sleeping pills, and then let her stage the scene for the discovery of what she intended to be construed as Mr. Wallings' suicide. That way, we could prevent her from claiming the whole thing was simply an accident." He considered the couch for a moment, then dragged a straight back chair over from a corner of the room, took a seat, and began pouring out tea and handing around cups. As he handed me a teacup and saucer he said, "I didn't get your messages until just now. I had my phone turned off. Couldn't have it ringing unexpectedly while I was hiding in the pantry."

"I see. Sorry for barging in."

Quimby opened his mouth to say something, but Mr. Wallings said, "Quite all right, my dear. Knowing that a pair of young people came to rescue me goes a long way in restoring my faith in human nature."

Quimby didn't look as if he agreed with the sentiment, but took a sip of his tea instead of speaking.

Alex put his cup in his saucer and leaned forward. "How did you expect to fool Eve? Mr. Wallings wasn't even drugged. He was only pretending to be asleep. If she'd checked his pulse, wouldn't the game be up?"

"He was supposed to be lightly drugged, but apparently, Mr. Wallings has built up some resistance to the medicine. Fortunately, we enlisted help, Jacob MacNamerra." Quimby pointed his teacup in the direction of the French windows where a police officer was escorting Sherry away from the young man, who stood alone, watching her go with a look of disgust on his face.

"The gardener?"

"Yes," Quimby said. "He witnessed the new will that Eve had Mr. Wallings sign when he was so woozy that he didn't know what he was doing, but once Jacob learned of Eve's plan to stage Mr. Wallings' suicide, he came to us. Jacob says that Eve convinced him to witness the will, saying that Mr. Wallings was really ill and not expected to live much longer. She promised to pay him several thousand pounds when she received her bequest."

"But wouldn't he have known Mr. Walling's true condition?"

"He wasn't in the house at all, didn't see me even once during the first months he worked here," Mr. Wallings said.

"Signing a piece of paper was one thing, but murder, well, he drew the line there," Quimby said. "He came to us last night and told us the whole plan. He agreed to work with us to bring in Eve and Sherry in exchange for immunity. Eve had told him it would be his job to check on Mr. Wallings, while she washed up the dishes and prepared the scene. He would simply check on Mr. Wallings then declare he was dead. We did the makeup in case Eve insisted on looking herself."

"But I knew she wouldn't touch me," Mr. Wallings said. "Evie doesn't like to touch people. Very odd, that, but there it is."

"How strange," I said, "but you know, thinking back to that day when she found us with you in the garden, she didn't touch you, even when she wanted you to go in the house."

Mr. Wallings nodded. "Yes. Beatrice noticed it, too, a while back. Mentioned it to me once, saying she thought Evie's hands-off manner was unusual. I hadn't noticed it myself until then, but it was true. When I was weak, she had a nurse in to help me. Evie never did any of the nursing herself." He stared down into his teacup. "Evie always was a bit of an odd duck, even as a child. Never happy."

Quimby cleared his throat and set his teacup down. "If you're feeling up to it, Ms. Sharp, I'd like to get a few details from you and Mr. Norcutt about how you came to be here today."

"Yes, of course." I put my teacup and saucer down. While Quimby was occupied with taking out his phone and tapping on the screen, I tried to think of the best way to explain the whole convoluted thing. "It goes back to Kevin. Funny, all this," I waved my hand toward the doorway where police officers were passing back and forth, "has pushed thoughts of Kevin into the background, but it goes back to him. I guess the best place to start is with the straps on the audio guides at Parkview Hall."

I went on to explain what I'd seen and how it reminded me of the way Kevin's camera strap had been folded. I came clean, recounting how I'd removed the camera from the box to get the memory card. By the time I'd finished, my cheeks were burning, and Quimby was frowning deeply. I'd already confessed to Olney about removing the memory card, but I felt even worse now, knowing that my interference prevented the police from getting what may have been an essential clue that could link Eve to Kevin.

I braced for a reprimand, but Quimby only shook his head. "Go on."

Feeling as if I'd gotten a reprieve, I went on to explain my conversation with Beatrice. "So then I knew Eve had lied. She told me she found out about Kevin's interest in Coventry House the day before, but she'd had a conversation with Beatrice about it a week before. I had even more questions, but they all got pushed to the side when Alex told me who Sherry was. I'd never seen her here as the cook, but then I saw her talking to...Jacob, wasn't it? That's when I recognized them as the couple from the river. Anyway, seeing them together made several odd things fall into a pattern that frightened me."

I recounted everything: the conversation about Jacob feeling guilty, Beatrice's sleepiness, Celia looking for a new job, the mortar and pestle in the kitchen but Sherry not knowing how to use them, Eve telling Sherry to stay away from the house until two, overhearing Eve say it would be "over by then," the quick word between Sherry and Jacob, and how they'd checked their watches. "Each thing individually didn't seem significant—important nothings—Austen would call them, but when I put them all together..." I stopped, not wanting to think about the horrible feeling that I'd had when everything fell into place. "Anyway, I hoped I was wrong, but if I wasn't..." I shrugged. "I called you, got your voicemail. When I couldn't find Beatrice, I had to come on my own."

"You arrived on foot?"

"Yes, my car was blocked in at Parkview House. Alex showed me the footpath. We even called an ambulance. Did it ever arrive?"

Quimby sighed. "Emergency checked with us before dispatching it. We'd briefed the local authorities on our sting, but by the time I got the word that some helpful citizen had called for an ambulance, you two were galloping up the stairs. If you had driven over and tried to come in the front gate, we would have prevented you from getting in. I had a man remotely operating the gate controls. He was to let Sherry and Jacob in, but no one else. I never thought that someone would come through the woods. I think we're done for now. I'll need each of you to give an official statement. We'll be in touch." Quimby tucked his phone into his pocket and stood.

Alex and I stood as well. Slink dragged herself to her feet, then shook her body in a movement that rippled from her head down to her tail. We said goodbye to Mr. Wallings then followed Quimby into the entry. He opened the door, revealing fat raindrops arrowing onto the gravel sweep.

"Let me get you lifts." Quimby motioned to a police officer standing in the hallway, and in short order, we had been sorted —me into one police car and Alex and Slink into another. We barely had time to exchange a wave through the rain-blurred car windows before we were efficiently swept away from Coventry House.

CHAPTER 21

*I*T RAINED ON AND OFF for the next two days, the sky heavy and dark, a fitting atmosphere for the inquest into Kevin's death. His body had been released and loaded onto a plane yesterday for transport back to the States. Eve was in custody, facing a myriad of charges, which ranged from fraud all the way up to attempted murder. Quimby had called to tell me a search of Eve's computer showed she had created profiles and posted on Internet forums, hoping to generate suspicion that someone in our office wanted Kevin out of the way, which would keep suspicion away from her.

The police had also found a fuzzy security recording from a merchant across the street from the crosswalk where I was pushed. While not conclusive, the images showed a woman, her face obscured by a hat, who came close to me. Her furled umbrella tangled with my ankles seconds before I fell. By the time I was on the ground, the woman had moved away. Using the streetlight and a nearby sign as a reference, the police had been able to work out that the woman was the exact height as Eve Wallings. The incident was minor compared to the other charges Eve faced, and it didn't look as if the police would be able to pursue any charges because they couldn't definitively link Eve to it, but after seeing the video, I had no doubt about what had happened.

I had expected to talk to Alex. We were supposed to meet one day for lunch, but he had to cancel. The only other thing I heard from him was a short text, asking how I was doing. I caught a glimpse of him after the inquest, but we hadn't talked face-to-face.

This morning, the day of my departure, had dawned clear and bright. I decided to walk down to the bridge. My suitcase was packed and my boarding pass printed. The streets of Nether Woodsmoor were damp, and once I was out of the village and on the footpath to the bridge, the trees glistened with water, an occasional drop smacking onto my shoulders. The very air seemed scrubbed clean and sparkly with a sharp, fresh scent.

I paused at the little clearing where Alex had stopped his car the day Kevin was found. I was glad to see the bridge was deserted. I followed the curving path around through the thickening wood and up the incline, then came out on the road. I walked to the center of the bridge, found a fairly dry spot on the golden stone, leaned my arms on it, and watched the water flow by in a steady current.

I stood there a long time, thinking about Kevin. A family passed by on the bridge, consulting a map, and talking about gardens, so I assumed they were going to Parkview Hall. A little later, a car lumbered slowly along, but the bridge was wide and had accommodated foot traffic as well as wheeled vehicles for hundreds of years. There was plenty of room, and I didn't have to move. Drivers here were used to sharing the road with walkers and bike-riders with no problems...well, except for Kevin, but his case was different. He had been targeted.

I heard another car approach, and looked up when the

engine didn't stay at the same steady rumble and pass me. The car, a red MG, turned off the road and stopped in the open area at the end of the bridge where Kevin had parked his car. Alex climbed out and crossed the bridge, his hands in his pockets, a tentative smile on his face. "Hey," he said.

"Hey. Where's Slink?"

"I had to leave her at home today." Alex leaned on the stones beside me. "I stopped by the inn. Doug told me you checked out today."

"Yes. My flight is this afternoon."

"I see."

We stood there a few minutes, the only sound, the water swooshing along beneath us.

"Are you okay? You got the details from Quimby, about Kevin, didn't you?"

I sighed and looked back at the water. "Yes. Eve says she didn't mean to hit him, just scare him. Quimby says there was impact damage to her car at the front bumper and at the edge of the windshield. They came back and examined the whole bridge and found traces of Kevin's DNA on the edge of the stone."

I stopped and cleared my throat. "Quimby showed me a sketch of what they think happened. Eve, angry with him about interfering with her plans, saw Kevin walking on the bridge. With his car in the water, he would have to cross it to return to Nether Woodsmoor. She accelerated and clipped his thigh. The impact broke his leg and threw him into the air. He hit the side of the car first, then the momentum carried him through the air to the side of the bridge. The back of his head connected with the balustrade of the bridge as he fell. Quimby says their medical people are sure he was at least unconscious, if not already gone, by the time he hit the water." I blew out a long breath.

"I'm sorry, Kate."

Unable to speak for a moment, I nodded, then finally said, "At least we know what really happened."

"And Becca was telling the truth," Alex said in a wondering tone. "Never would have thought that."

I couldn't help but smile and glance at Alex. I had to look away again quickly. There was something about the way he focused on me, seeming to listen with his whole face, that made me feel elated and slightly nervous at the same time.

"I'm sorry I've been MIA for the last two days," he said. "I had a—well, a family emergency, then I got word about a new project."

"It's okay," I said quickly. "So you've got something else lined up. That's good because Marci says the prospects of *P & P* getting made are less than zero right now. It's all over except for the official announcement. Funding trouble. Sorry," I said, knowing the loss of the job would impact his finances, which Quimby had pointed out weren't all that solid.

"It's fine. Don't worry about me. I'll get by. I always do. What will you do?"

"I'm not sure. I could always go out on my own, but I don't know if I want to do that. I'm not as…hungry and aggressive as Kevin."

"You could always move to another firm—" He broke off at the sound of a dog barking. Two small bundles of fur emerged from the path on the side of the bridge near Parkview Hall. Beatrice held the taut leashes as the two dogs yapped their way across the bridge and joined us.

"Hush," she commanded, but the dogs only calmed down after Alex and I petted them. "Have to keep them on a leash now that we're open again." Beatrice addressed the dogs. "You lot are horribly behaved. Embarrassing."

The dogs had stopped barking, but continued to twist in and out around us, tangling their leashes. "So distressing, this whole thing with Eve. Trying to murder her uncle. Positively Machiavellian."

"How is Mr. Wallings?"

"Improving every day. He's still quite upset at what happened—doesn't show it, but Harold and I can tell. We will keep an eye on him. I predict that Edwin will be walking without a cane by the end of summer. So I suppose you're off to the States soon?" Beatrice asked.

"Today, and I'm afraid I won't be back. Looks as if the movie isn't going to happen after all." I hated to be the bearer of bad news, but projects did fall through, and it wasn't the first time I had to do it.

"That's a shame," Beatrice said with perfect equanimity. "Would have been a coup for Nether Woodsmoor, but there you go. You probably can't wait to get out of our little village, having seen the dark side of it."

"L.A. is pretty dark at times, too. No, I will miss it here." I didn't mean to look at Alex as I said the words, but I couldn't help letting my glance slide his way a bit.

"I won't keep you," Beatrice said, working to untangle the leashes, which now resembled a braided rope.

"Here, let me," Alex said and went to work.

"Thank you." Beatrice patted the pockets of her cardigan. "Now you must let me take your picture. I'll put it in the drawing room and tell visitors about my brush with Hollywood."

"Oh, I don't know."

"Just like a photographer. Never like having their own picture taken." She shooed me into the center of the bridge and snapped a few photos. Alex handed her the untangled leashes. "Thank you," Beatrice said. "Now, go on, join her. I don't have a decent snap of you either." Beatrice gave him a firm push in my direction. "Put your arm around her. Closer."

Alex's arm went around my shoulder, his clean soapy scent enveloping me.

"Yes. That's lovely."

Beatrice lowered the phone, and we broke apart. "I'll send you both copies. I'm sure it's like the cobbler's children and their shoes. You probably don't have any photos of yourself. All right I'm off. I can't tolerate goodbyes. I hope you come back for a visit someday, Kate." She tugged on the leashes and the dogs stopped circling and sniffing and dashed off at full speed down the road.

"What time is your flight? Do you have time for lunch?" Alex asked.

I looked at my watch. "No, I have to go, this moment, in fact. I have to get back to the inn."

"I'll drive you." We hopped in the car. There wasn't time to clean out the passenger seat. I sat on a few pages of paper and some sticky notes, and Alex had me back at the inn within a few minutes. "Let me know about *P & P*, will you?"

"Of course."

As FLIGHTS GO, my return flight wasn't bad. It was a normal international flight, which meant I arrived back in L.A. exhausted and bleary-eyed. I walked out of the airport into a wall of dry, hot air and immediately stripped off my jacket, pushed up my sleeves, and dug in my bag for my sunglasses. I squinted against the piercing glare of the sun as I made my way to my car. I'd been away so long I had to bring up the picture I'd snapped on my phone of the aisle and row where I'd parked —a little trick I'd learned from Kevin. I sighed, sad that I would never have the opportunity to thank him for teaching me the ropes of location scouting. I found my car, drove straight home, and slept for thirteen hours.

When I woke up the next day, I texted Marci, letting her know I was back in town and on my way to the office. There was a wreck on the interstate, and it took me thirty minutes to cover half a mile. Breathing exhaust fumes from the cars in front of me and moving forward in inch-length increments, I thought of the quiet, narrow roads around Nether Woodsmoor and fuzzy white sheep dotting the rolling hills.

I scanned the horizon as I crept forward: triple lines of brake lights burning red, graffiti on the concrete overpass, and, in the distance through the thin haze of smog, the sharp angles of metal and glass buildings. It wasn't exactly a picture post-card view.

I finally got through the bottleneck and arrived at the office to find a 'For Lease' sign tucked into the frosted glass pane that ran alongside the door. The lights in the front office area were dark.

I flicked them on. "Marci?" Her desk was completely clear, and the bookcase behind her desk was empty.

Marci's silhouette with her distinctive spiky hair appeared in Kevin's doorway. "Hey, you're back." She carried a heavy cardboard box to the front door and set it beside a stack of similar boxes, which were labeled: ACCOUNTS RECEIVABLE, CLIENT LEADS, and LEGAL.

"So it's true? We're out of business?"

"Afraid so. Got the official word from Mr. O'Leery's people that the *P & P* project had been cancelled, and we've been getting cancellation calls for the last few days from our other clients. Without Kevin, they're moving on to someone else."

"Ah." I went to my desk, which already had two flattened cardboard boxes leaning against it. I dropped my tote bag into the chair and picked up a box. I flexed the cardboard flaps into place. "What happened to Lori?" I asked, tilting my head toward the empty plain of her desk. Her pink and white polka dot pencil cup and file holder were gone, and the wall behind her desk where the *Pride and Prejudice* movie posters had hung was blank.

"She decided last week she wants to be a Zumba instructor."

"Hmm. Well, she always was a bit obsessed about the crunches versus sit-up debate." I slapped a length of tape along the seam of the cardboard flaps and flipped the box over.

"What about Zara? I bet she was the first one out of here."

"Yes, she's like a cat. She always lands on her feet. She's moving to New York. Apparently, those personal days she took were for a job interview not to sort out something with her ex."

"So she *wasn't* in Chicago," I said, thinking of those few crazy moments when I suspected that Zara might have flown to England.

"What did you say?"

"Oh, nothing important." I nestled my ivy plant in a corner of the box, as I asked, "How are you doing?"

"Surprisingly okay. I'm still upset over what happened to Kevin, but the reality of him being gone has sunk in. I'm sorry they wouldn't hold the funeral for another day so you could attend."

"It's all right. I said goodbye to him in England," I said, thinking about my last visit to the bridge. Kevin's funeral had been held on the day I flew back.

"A distant cousin of Kevin's showed up and his two ex-wives." Marci disappeared into Kevin's office for more boxes. "Everyone else was a work associate. TMZ sent some cameramen, who hovered outside the funeral home in hopes of getting a shot of Mr. O'Leary, but he sent flowers instead."

"Sounds like it was a bit of a circus."

"Yes. Kevin would have loved it." She dropped the box on the stack by the door. "I'm going to work for Karen James," Marci said, naming one of our top competitors.

"That's great. I'm glad you've found something." I put my

glass paperweight and the brass clock I'd picked up on a scouting trip to San Francisco in the box, then wound my extra phone charging cord into a circle. "You don't sound excited, though."

"Well, it's that—I feel bad. Karen said she could take me on. Her office manager quit two months ago, and she's had a series of temps who have apparently been atrocious. It will probably take me until Thanksgiving just to straighten out the receivables, but she doesn't need another location scout right now. She said if they expand, she might need someone else after the New Year."

"Marci, under that prickly exterior you are such a softie. It's not up to you to find me a job, too. Just take care of yourself. I'll find something."

She half grinned. "Don't let on to anyone who works for Karen. I have a whole new group of people to whip into shape and that's a lot easier to do if everyone is afraid of me."

"Your secret is safe with me."

Marci carried out another box, and I cleared out my top drawer. How had I missed the three tubes of Smarties? If I'd known those were in there, they would have been eaten long ago.

"Oh." Marci appeared in Kevin's doorway, a box weighing down her arms. "I forgot. Leon called when he heard we were shutting down. He said he'd be interested in talking to you. So that's a lead, you know. A possibility," she said, her voice uncharacteristically tentative. "He's doing well. He's landed several feature film projects recently. It could be a good move for you. He'd hire you in a heartbeat. I know that."

I wrinkled my nose. "Lip-licking Leon? No thanks." For some reason, our colleague Leon Bettis found my collarbones fascinating. Every time I ran into him, he couldn't seem to keep his gaze above my chin, and he had a habit of frequent lip licking.

"That's what I thought you'd say. I told him you already had some leads."

"Thanks."

It didn't take long to finish boxing my personal things and transfer them to my car, then I spent the rest of the afternoon helping Marci with Kevin's office. It was close to five by the time we finished. We made one final sweep, and that's when I saw Kevin's antique camera sitting on the window ledge tucked behind the vertical blinds. He had kept it on the credenza behind his desk. "Marci, don't forget Kevin's Brownie camera."

"Oh, I'm so glad you saw that. He wanted you to have it."

"What?"

"I found a copy of his will in the legal paperwork. He wanted you to have the Brownie camera."

I turned the camera over in my hands. "That's so…"

"Unlike him? Sentimental?" Marci said.

"I was going to say it was so nice of him."

"Yeah, it was." Marci dusted her hands on her hips. "I think we're done here."

She locked the door, and we walked to the parking garage together, making plans to meet for lunch. I slid into the car, started it up, and sat there a moment, letting the air conditioner blast me with cool air as I ran my fingers over the worn corners of the boxy camera.

My phone buzzed with a text from Beatrice. *As promised.* The photo of Alex and me on the bridge was attached. As I studied the photo, a call came in. It was Alex.

I put the Brownie camera carefully in the cardboard box between the gargoyle replica I'd picked up in Paris and pile of Moleskines, and considered letting the call go to voicemail, but at the last moment, I answered.

"Hey, you made it back. How was your flight?" Alex asked.

"Long and boring."

"Ah. Well, that's better than short and exciting, I guess."

"I've never thought of it that way, but that's true. I do have some bad news."

"The movie's off," Alex said unemotionally.

"You guessed it. You don't sound too upset."

"No. I'm sorry that it's fallen through."

"It's not unexpected though," I summed up. "Right. Well, I hope you're not left high and dry."

"No. No, I'm not. In fact—remember that project I mentioned? The one I had to cancel our lunch for? It's a go."

"That's great." I managed not to say that I was currently jobless.

"Yeah, the work is great, but the thing is…" his voice trailed off, and I thought we'd lost the connection, but then his voice came back stronger. He hurried through his next words as if he wanted to get them out there. "I need someone else. It's a huge project with a short timeline, and I know you work in L.A. and all, but I was wondering if you'd consider coming out here for a month or two and working with me. I know I'm asking you to return to a place with sad memories, but I'd hoped that…"

"Not all my memories of Nether Woodsmoor are sad," I said slowly.

"Um…yeah. Well, before you turn me down flat, let me tell you about the project. It's for a cable network, a biographical look at Jane Austen. The producer heard about my link to Mr. Dunn's project, and thought I might be able to help her move quickly because of all the preliminary work I've done."

"It's about Jane Austen, but it's not an adaptation of one of her books," I said to make sure I understood.

"Right. It's more of an overview, a look at her life and her novels. The producer wants actors recreating scenes from Austen's life and from some of the books. Interviews with literary experts will be interspersed throughout the piece, and it will have an analysis of the pop culture aspect of her fame. So you see, it would be helpful to have someone with a good knowledge of Jane Austen's novels and the Regency. I know it would mean more travel for you and more time away from home, but I hope you'll consider it." He paused, then said in a quieter voice, "I'd like to work with you again."

I was parked on the top deck of the parking garage at the very edge and had a view of a slice of grayish sky between two office towers. I studied their sleek monolithic glassed sides reflecting images of each other as I thought about his offer. I could turn him down, stay here. Search out a new position as a location scout or go freelance.

"You don't have to decide right now. Take some time. Think about it."

My gaze dropped down to the ground floor of the buildings where office workers streamed out of the revolving doors, briskly striding in ant-like lines to the crosswalk or the parking garages, their briefcases swinging, phones pressed to their ears. I thought of the stop-and-go drive home, the barbed wire twisted around the freeway signs to discourage graffiti and the dry hills covered in scrub and manzanita that I couldn't see beyond the gray wall of haze.

Smog, traffic, and no job versus golden stone cottages, rolling green fields, and a paycheck. "No, I don't have to think about it. It sounds excessively diverting."

"I hoped you'd say that."

THE END

THE STORY BEHIND THE STORY

Kate and Alex will return in another adventure. Let me know if you'd like to read more of their stories. You can sign up for my newsletter at SaraRosett.com/signup/2 for exclusive excerpts of upcoming books and member-only giveaways. If you've enjoyed *Death in the English Countryside* and feel inclined to post an on-line review, I'd appreciate it. Posting an honest reader review is one of the best ways to help authors. Thanks!

I am neither a Jane Austen scholar nor a location scout, so the research for this book was both interesting and challenging.

Like Kate, I adore *Pride and Prejudice*. I reread it as I wrote *Death in the English Countryside*, and found *Pride and Prejudice* to be even more delightful than I remembered it—indeed, I did.

Viewing the recent adaptions of *P & P* was hard work, but I absolutely *had* to do it. *Jane Austen's World: The Life and Times of England's Most Popular Novelist* by Maggie Lane and *Jane Austen: The World of Her Novels* by Deirdre Le Fay provided a fascinating insight into Austen's life, times, and writings.

I traveled to Derbyshire and experienced the green sheep-dotted hills and stunning country homes, loving every minute of it. Take a look at my *Death in the English Countryside* pinboard to see places that inspired me.

Hannah Dennison graciously clued me in on custards, puddings, and gave me tips on UK police procedure. I also spent quite a bit of time curled up with *The Crime Writer's Guide to Police Practice and Procedure* by Michael O'Byrne.

Because *Death in the English Countryside* is first and foremost a mystery, I've streamlined some of the location scouting details for the sake of story and plot. For an in-depth look at how a period drama is made, I highly recommend Sue Birtwistle and Susie Conklin's book, *The Making of Pride and Prejudice.*

ABOUT THE AUTHOR

A native Texan, Sara is the author of the Ellie Avery mystery series and the *On The Run* suspense series. As a military spouse, Sara has moved around the country (frequently!) and traveled internationally, which inspired her latest suspense novels. *Publishers Weekly* called Sara's books, "satisfying," "well-executed," and "sparkling."

Sara loves all things bookish, considers dark chocolate a daily requirement, and is on a quest for the best bruschetta. Get exclusive content and new release updates from Sara at Sara-Rosett.com/signup/2.

Connect with Sara
www.SaraRosett.com

OTHER BOOKS BY SARA

THIS IS SARA ROSETT'S COMPLETE library at the time of publication, but Sara has new books coming out all the time. Sign up for her newsletter at SaraRosett.com/signup/2 to stay up to date on new releases.

Murder on Location

Death in the English Countryside

Death in an English Cottage

Death in a Stately Home

Death in an Elegant City

Menace at the Christmas Market (novella)

Death in an English Garden

Death at an English Wedding

On the Run

Elusive

Secretive

Deceptive

Suspicious

Devious

Treacherous

Ellie Avery

Moving is Murder

Staying Home is a Killer

Getting Away is Deadly

Magnolias, Moonlight, and Murder

Mint Juleps, Mayhem, and Murder
Mimosas, Mischief, and Murder
Mistletoe, Merriment and Murder
Milkshakes, Mermaids, and Murder
Marriage, Monsters-in-law, and Murder
Mother's Day, Muffins, and Murder